MORS DEI

Expansions of the Mind

Zoë LeCraw

Mors Dei

tellwell

Tellwell Talent
www.tellwell.ca

ISBN
978-1-77302-944-3 (Hardcover)
978-1-77302-943-6 (Paperback)
978-1-77302-945-0 (eBook)

Acknowledgments

Writing has always been a part of life, but it wasn't until a certain someone, the beautiful Kristen Kerr, kicked my ass into motivational gear that I got really serious with it, and I'll always be thankful for that. You helped to turn my life around right at the perfect time, and I'll forever be grateful to you for that.

Also, thank you to all my friends, family, and co-workers who have been so supporting throughout this entire journey. Whether by being the first person to read my preliminary work for this book, Carleigh Warburton, and being so excited to read more. Or by providing me with everything I could ever need and more, my wonderful Mum Sally Blake. By teaching me how to social media and helping to get my name out there, Elizabeth Klatt. Or by being there for many needed wine nights and coffee dates, Dalandrea Adams.

To everyone who's asked, "How's your book coming along?", "When does it come out?", "When do I get my signed copy ;)?", thank you for showing your interest and support, and thank you for keeping me excited about my future.

Thank you! <3

The world as we know it...

08-23-2087: The Day the Earth Drowned...

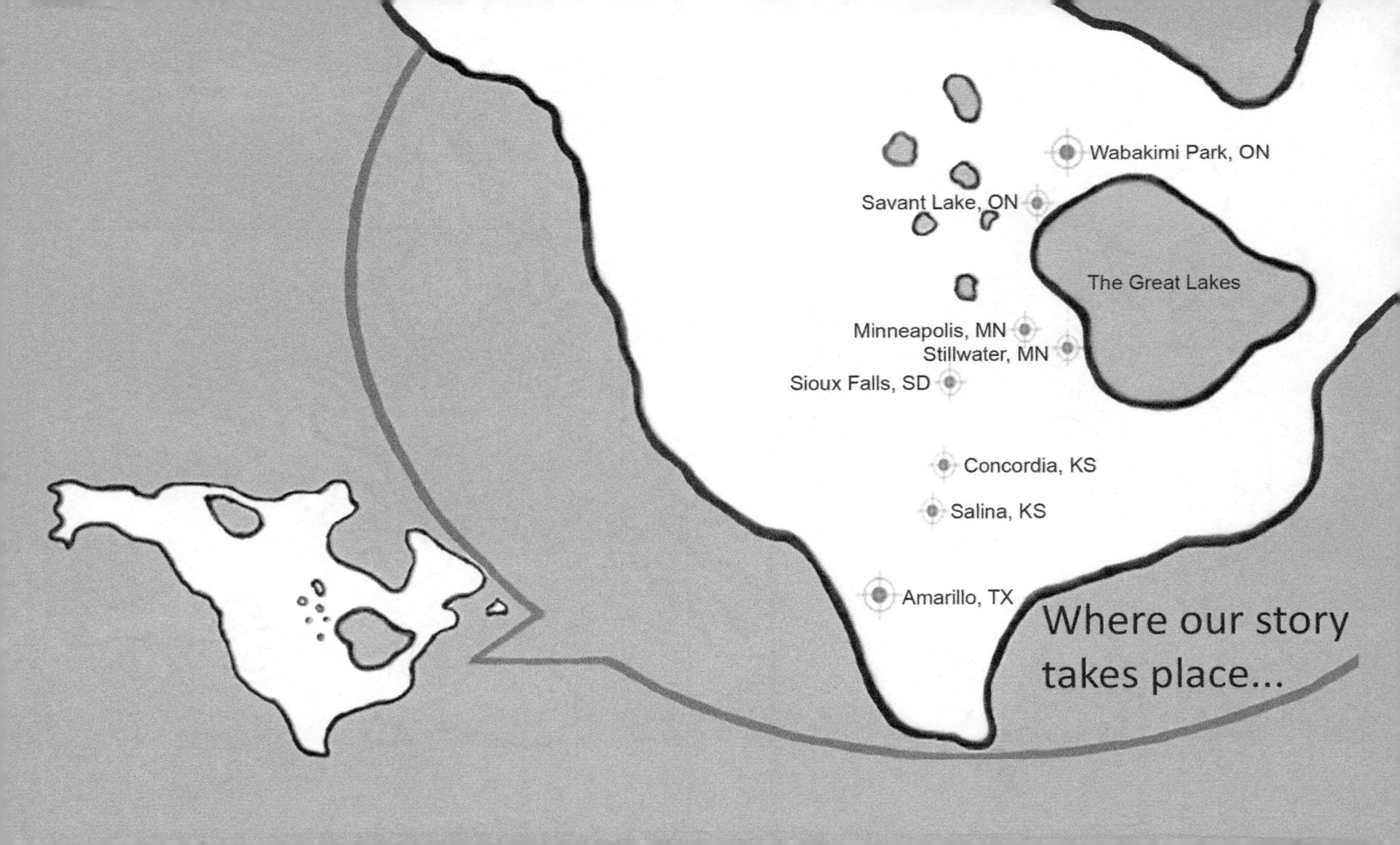
Wabakimi Park, ON
Savant Lake, ON
The Great Lakes
Minneapolis, MN
Stillwater, MN
Sioux Falls, SD
Concordia, KS
Salina, KS
Amarillo, TX
Where our story takes place...

Prologue

08-23-2087: The Day the Earth Drowned. It is one that reset all history books. The 'End of Days' to end all 'End of Days'. Predicted, but unpreventable. Scientists of the joined governments of Canada and the United States found that there was to be a double solar flare event that would blast the Arctic and Antarctic at once, leading to significant water level changes. They had tried to pinpoint a date to the event, but as unpredictable as normal weather patterns are, abnormal ones are even more uncertain. Warnings were issued instructing people who lived near the shore to move inland, and they did, but the imminent global flood would be greater than they ever thought possible.

There was hearsay of underwater bunkers being built for people to flee to when the catastrophe did strike, but the rumors were never confirmed. And when the flares finally came, the Earth was scorched and drowned in one fell swoop. The repercussions were catastrophic, and the loss of life was as substantial as the loss of land and resources. Beautiful national parks were burnt to a crisp, turning the luscious green earth into a dusty barren wasteland. The trees were decimated, and those that did survive the blast became great corpses of the magnificence they once exuded. Cities came crumbling down, leaving in its wake a ruin that was nothing more than a pile of rubble, while beautiful countrysides were swallowed whole by the remorseless waters.

Lake clusters became small oceans within the remaining land masses as the pressure of the rushing waters burst forth, and across the globe pockets of earth came rocketing up from deep below, leaving tiny ponds scattered across the scorched earth.

Amid all the death and destruction rose a man who thought he could change the world; even before the disaster occurred this was his belief. So while everyone else was picking themselves back up, and with the government nowhere to be found, he provided them with structure, and someone to look to for leadership. Unfortunately, it would be too late before they realized the maniac he truly was.

Most had heard of his work under the name 'Project Deus'. But none knew the true horrors that lay within it, and no one could imagine the extreme lengths he was willing to go to prove his theories were possible now that he had free reign.

With the last of humanity under his thumb one woman, Aiyana Waki, rose up to bring together an army in the hopes to end his tyranny. As word of this reached his facility several of his subjects planned, and managed, to escape. In an attempt to retrieve his legacies, and put an end to her rebel army, he unleashed a horde of bio-mechanical creatures of his own creation.

Chapter 1

The high-pitched ringing in her ears had become a constant in her life, while sleep seemed fleeting and infrequent. But somehow she kept going, kept fighting. The war against these unknown abominations had been going on for three years now, and it seemed there was no end in sight. But she couldn't give up.

The sounds of gunfire and explosions had dwindled into such normality that their constant presence had become a white noise; even the screams of her fellow comrades were beginning to blend into that white noise. It was only the distinct sound of one her friends being ripped apart that still made her heart lurch out of her chest. She had learned to ignore the desire to run in the direction of that terrible scream to find out who it was, to see if they could still be saved. They never could.

While all these sounds had slowly blurred into obscurity, the sound of the enemy was forever cringe-worthy.

The sound of metal grinding and screeching against itself, combined with the slickness of moist flesh, never failed to make her skin crawl and her heart pound faster.

She knew Dean was out there somewhere, fighting for his life just like the others, and though she ached to reach out to him she knew that to do so could have catastrophic consequences. They had tried fighting side by side, but they'd learned that fighting together only made it more dangerous.

Dean jumped from a piece of metal that was jutting up out of the ground, the angle of elevation allowing his landing to come down right on top of one of the vicious biomechanical creatures. The creature tried to swing Dean off of its large, bulbous body, but with no luck. Dean held on to where its mechanical limbs met with its fleshy parts with strong arms, the handle of his knife clenched between his teeth, waiting for the opportune moment to strike. The creature made a screeching sound and tilted backward to try and throw the man from its back, but he held on. Dean watched as one of its limbs came flying backward, and he grabbed ahold of it just in time causing the creature to tumble to the side. Dean grabbed the knife from his mouth, and plunged it deep into the creatures neck, then rolled away taking the knife with him. Hot gray slime oozed from the creatures wound as it spasmed from the injury. Dean scanned the area, making sure there were no other incoming creatures, before sheathing his knife. He then dove into the mass of writhing flesh and metal, forced his hand into the gushing wound, and grasped what would compare to a spine. After getting a firm grip he ripped a chunk of spine out of the creature's body, and the metal limbs went limp, losing their connection to its brain. Its lidless eyes darted back and forth, and its large mouth snapped and snarled with massive teeth, but was unable to do anything else.

"Well you're a nasty piece of work aren't you?" Dean said tauntingly.

He looked up at the horizon while wiping sweat from his brow, the sky was dimming with the beginnings of dusk. The creature continued its snarling, and let out a vicious howl.

"Oh shut up."

Dean fired a small handgun, shooting a tranquilizer dart into the creature's face. The snarling ceased, and he scanned the area once more for any incoming enemies, of which there were none, then unsheathed his knife and began hacking away at the flesh surrounding the mechanical limbs. As he removed the last limb the sun had almost set, and he knew he had to get back to the base soon. He gripped onto two lumps within the fleshy mass and began to drag it back, leaving the metal appendages behind.

Dean thought of Kaia and wanted to reach out to her, but she could still be fighting, and he didn't want to break her concentration. So he poured all of his focus into dragging the body of the creature back home. He hoped that a dissection of it might help them discover more about them: where they came from, who created them, what their purpose was, why they came after himself and Kaia with more ferocity than the others, and most importantly, how to kill them. For good.

Kaia jumped from one of the metal limbs of the creature she was fighting and slid across the cracked and dusty, blood-stained ground. The body of the creature went limp and came crashing down beside her. She could already hear the whirring and clicking inside of it that would bring it back to life again tomorrow. Kaia looked out at the setting sun and knew she needed to get back to base now, hopefully Dean would be there waiting for her.

Kaia jogged at a steady pace, keeping her eyes peeled for enemy movement. As she got closer to the base she passed by some of the night crew heading out into the field. Every one of them nodded at her as they passed by, signaling their respect for her authority as one of two General-Heads; the other being Dean. Kaia jogged through the entrance of the base, stopping to speak to the four Captains on guard duty -two of which would be leaving soon. Payne, Barnes, Darkholme, and Adler.

Benjamin Payne and Freddie Barnes were both men of tall and athletic stature, and were close friends that could easily pass for brothers. Their defining differences were that Ben had shaggy brown hair and dark brown eyes, while Freddie had blonde hair and light brown eyes. Samantha Darkholme and Hannah Adler appeared as polar opposites, but were, in fact, closer than a pair of cannibal midgets in a fat guy's rib cage -as Ben would say. Sam was a short, fit woman with pixie-cut black hair and blue eyes that shone brightly, while Hannah was almost a foot taller than Sam, and had green eyes and long blonde hair that was always pulled back into a ponytail.

"Has Dean come back yet?" She asked.

"Not yet General Whittaker. You should go inside. I'll let him know you're here when he returns."

"I will Ben, just a few more minutes."

The five of them stood in silence, looking out over the sad state the land had become. Aiyana had found this old military base hidden deep within Wabakimi Park shortly before the disaster, and turned it into the fully functioning building it is now in the hopes to build a sanctuary for survivors. When she first discovered the place beautiful landscapes had kept it hidden from view:

massive trees, ponds, and beautiful greenery had covered the land. Now it was like looking out at an old dried up prairie with scattered corpses of only the most massive of oak trees. Everything else had been turned ash during the flares.

Just as Kaia was about to walk in she saw in the distance a man dragging something large behind him.

"Ben, Freddie, will you help that-"

Kaia stopped speaking as soon as she realized who it was, and sprinted across the distance between herself and Dean.

Dean!

Dean looked up, blinking the sweat out of his eyes.

Kaia! What are you doing?

Coming to help you. What is... Kaia stopped mid-sentence as she saw what was coming up over the hill behind Dean.

Dean! Run!

Dean looked behind him to see the largest creature he'd ever seen since the war had started and redoubled his effort in dragging the incapacitated creature back to base.

"Captains! Suppressing fire. Now!" She yelled, pointing to the creature.

The four were already advancing as they peered down the scopes of their guns, and began firing at the massive thing. Kaia ran ahead of them, sprinting as fast as she could while ensuring she wasn't in their firing path. As Kaia reached Dean she didn't falter for a second, immediately thrusting her hands into the fleshy mass and grabbing ahold of it. While pulling the creature along, with just as much effort as her other half, Kaia brushed against Sam and shouted to the Captains to fall back. The four of them continued to shoot at the creature while retreating with their Generals, and it was beginning to slow down. The creature was using most of its limbs to deflect the bullets, but even only using half its limbs to run it still managed to cover a large amount of ground with every step. Ben saw Dean and Kaia approaching the doors of the base, and he sprinted back to get them open. Sam, Hannah, and Freddie, upon hearing the whooshing of the doors, turned around and ran back to safety. With the firing ceased the creature was able to use all of its limbs for one purpose, and it was quickly gaining on them.

Ben helped Kaia and Dean drag the creature through as the others raced for the open doors. Kaia looked back, blowing a strand of hair out of her eyes, and could see Ben firing his weapon again. Kaia ran up and joined him, firing her 9mm Glock into the creature's face.

The three Captains ran and dodged their way to the base, almost getting skewered a number of times. With seconds to spare they dove through the open doors, and Ben pulled Kaia back as he shut them. A loud thud was heard from the other side, and the doors shuddered. They all had their weapons aimed at the doors, and Dean quickly joined them with his own firearm; an S&W 500 Magnum. Several minutes passed by with nothing before they all sighed a breath of relief and lowered their weapons.

From behind them a sort of squishy sound began to creep up, then a snarl, then a growl. The six men and women turned around to see that the thing Dean had dragged back with him was trying to roll itself over to them -a ball of snapping teeth and flying spittle. Dean holstered his Magnum to pull out a small strange looking hand gun, and fired three more tranquilizers into its face.

"What is that?" Kaia asked.

"It's one of the creatures... you know, without its limbs." He grinned.

The four Captains shuffled their feet a little; a sign that they were anxious with that thing so close to them.

"Can three of you take this to Dr. Lee? And let her know I'll be by sometime tomorrow to speak with her." Kaia addressed the Captains.

Sam nodded and saluted, the other three following suit.

"Thank you." Kaia said.

The two Generals left through the only other door in the hallway, and as it closed behind them everyone noticed Freddie shaking his head with a disgusted look on his face.

"That thing looks like a giant spider body. I ain't going near it."

"What kind of freaky ass spiders came into your room as a kid?" Sam asked, humor in her voice.

Freddie looked at the unconscious creature with disgust and fear. Without all those robotic limbs it just reminded him of the spiders his late brother used to collect. Only much, much bigger, and with fewer eyes; although more terrifying considering their lidlessness.

"Yeah... I'll just wait here." Freddie half saluted, half waved goodbye as the three walked towards the creature.

Ben and the women chuckled, and as they lifted the heavy mass of the limbless creature they couldn't help but wonder how Dean had managed to drag it so far by himself.

Chapter 2

"Okay, I have to ask." Kaia said, swallowing the last bite of her dinner, "How did you dismember it like that?"

Dean took a gulp of water before responding, "It was easy once I was able to remove a piece of its spine." He spoke nonchalantly, and his eyes shone with the mischievousness of a child while the corner of his mouth lifted in a grin.

Kaia chuckled and sighed, "I miss fighting with you."

"I know. Me too," He reached across the table for her hand, "but you know what it was like when we were together out there."

"I know, I know. I just wish-"

I know. He responded in her mind, increasing the intimacy of emotion.

I love you.

I love you too.

The two finished their meal, then walked back to their room, each with the same thing on their mind.

As soon as the door was closed Dean pushed Kaia up against the wall, and kissed her hard on the mouth; Kaia returned the kiss just as passionately. Dean held her wrists up above her head with one hand while running the fingers of his other hand through her long, dark ginger hair, and pulling it out of its ponytail. Kaia pulled back from the kiss momentarily and looked into his emerald eyes. They were so bright that she could see the pale blue color of her own reflected in them. As his eyes bore into hers she began to quiver with ecstasy, and her knees became weak. He laughed a low, short laugh, one of enjoyment, and Kaia bit her lower lip teasingly. Dean immediately responded by kissing and gently nipping at her collarbone. Kaia let out a soft moan, and he let go of her wrists to kneel down in front of her. As Dean unzipped her pants his hair brushed lightly against the small area of skin that had been revealed on her stomach, and Kaia closed her eyes, quietly moaning again. Dean slowly pulled off each pant leg, taking pleasure at the sight of her toned legs, and as he came back up he grabbed the bottom of her shirt, lifting it up over her head to reveal an equally slim and toned body. Dean nuzzled into her collarbone, and she wrapped her arms around him, gripping the edges of his shirt. As he pulled back she pulled the shirt up over his head, revealing a magnificently muscled torso. A low gruff moan rumbled in Dean's throat as she lightly traced the lines of the muscles in his arms, in his chest, and in his abs, until she reached the waist of his pants. Dean's eyes rolled back in pleasure, and Kaia unzipped his pants, letting them fall to the floor. He then picked Kaia up by her buttocks and brought her to the bed where he pulled her bra off. Dean ran his hands up her stomach to her breasts, then lowered his mouth to one of her nipples, and she immediately let out a moan. Dean fed off of the sounds of pleasure escaping his wife's mouth and continued to tease her.

It soon became all sweat and naked bodies writhing within the thin sheets. When it was over they lay entwined with each other, breathing heavily, and with more than satisfied smiles on their faces. Kaia ran her fingers through his short hair -which was normally a hazel brunette, but was currently covered with the muck of the day- and lightly traced them down the side of his face.

"You're covered in dirt, and blood, and god knows what else."

Kaia let out a small laugh, and Dean took her hand, kissing it gently.

"Yeah, I probably should have showered before covering you in my grime, but I couldn't wait any longer."

"It's okay, me neither."

Kaia sighed happily and closed her eyes. Suddenly, an image flashed through her mind.

Dean, impaled on one of the creature's sharpened limbs. Blood dripping from his mouth. Freddie, pinned against a broken wall, guts spilling out of his abdomen, tumbling to the ground; a great shadow stepping over him. Electricity sparking. Hannah, eyes wide open but glazed over with death, bloody and limp. Sam, shirt ripped open, covered in blood, her remaining arm stretched out towards Hannah, blood gurgling out of her mouth as she sputtered her last breaths. Ben, legs gone, screaming; the shadow getting closer. Dean, reaching out for her. So much blood.

Kaia's eyes shot open to see Dean's face smiling down at her, his eyes crinkling with love, and his hands running through her hair.

"Is everything okay?" He asked.

"Mhmm." Kaia nodded, smiling back at him, forcing the sudden vision from her mind.

Chapter 3

The dull sound of someone knocking on their heavy door roused Kaia, and she looked towards it only to see darkness. She tilted her head up to try and see the small window that allowed the predawn light to filter through, but there was only more darkness. The knocking continued, and Dean grumbled while rolling over to bury his head in the pillow. Kaia disentangled her legs from Dean's and grabbed her watch off of the side table. 3:47 am. Kaia rubbed her eyes, both curious and annoyed to have been woken at such an hour. The knocking came again.

"Just a minute." She half shouted-half yawned at the door.

Kaia could hear feet shuffling, but at least the knocking stopped. Dean lifted himself up, letting out a huge yawn, and rubbed a hand along Kaia's leg. Kaia kissed him, climbed out of bed, and started to get dressed.

"What time is it?" Dean asked, grogginess still evident in his voice.

"Too early." Kaia said, pointing up at the small window, "I mean, nothing's exploding so I don't see why whatever it is couldn't have waited until the sun was up at least."

Dean laughed a little, sitting up on the edge of the bed and rubbing his head. As he stood up to get dressed with her, Kaia walked around to him and pressed herself up against his body. She breathed in deeply and leaned her head against his bare chest, enjoying the simplicity of the moment. Dean wrapped his arms around her and kissed the top of her head, and they stood there like that until the voice on the other side of the door broke the silence.

"Uh, Generals' Whittaker. We really do need you to see this."

The two sighed in unison and looked into each others eyes, love reflecting back at one another. Kaia went to go to the door, but Dean pulled her back for a quick kiss before letting her go. Kaia was smiling as she opened the door, but seeing Sam standing there with a worried look on her face diminished it.

"General Whittaker there's-"

"Please, Sam, we've known each other for as long as I've been here. You and Hannah are my closest friends, and you of all people have the right to call me Kaia."

Sam paused for a moment, then smiled. Kaia had saved her life on countless occasions in the field, and vice versa -even before her promotion to General.

"Kaia. There's something you and your husband should see. This way."

Dean was beside Kaia now, stretching his arms high up over his head, his fingers gripping the door frame.

"So, what's going on?"

"Come on." Kaia smiled, and they followed as Sam lead the way.

The Generals quickly recognized the path that they were taking was leading them to Dr. Seong Lee's office in Sector C; otherwise known as The Lab. They eventually came to a set of thick steel doors, and just inside was Hannah, along with Dr. Lee and three of her assistants.

"Thank you." Seong nodded at Sam, and the two women took their leave.

"Generals' Whittaker." Seong turned to face them, "This is Dr. Janna Grey, Dr. Gi Kyung, and Dr. Charles Hunt."

They all wore white lab coats with varying degrees of muck on them from the dissection of the creature, and they all looked exhausted. Seong was a tall, thin Japanese woman who had dark eyes to match equally dark hair. Hair that was pulled back into a messy bun that seemed strange in her otherwise strictly professional appearance of a skirt suit and plain black heels. Janna was a short and busty woman with curly, dirty blonde hair, and bright hazel eyes that shone behind thin, rectangular bright red glasses. Gi was a Korean man with buzz-cut hair and, impossibly, even darker eyes than Seong. And Charles was a tall, bald man who had enough signs of aging on his face to make you question his true age: lines etched into his forehead, and wrinkles near his eyes and mouth. Kaia and Dean shook each of their hands in turn.

"So what have you found?" Dean asked eagerly, hoping his dangerous plan had brought at least some good news.

"Some yes. As well as some bad news, and... well, peculiar news." Seong said.

Dean and Kaia shared a short look with raised eyebrows, then grabbed some stools that were by a desk, and sat down on them giving the four doctors all of their attention.

Seong spoke first, "We started by hooking the creature up to machines to monitor its vital signs and brain activity. To see and document how it would react to the dissections. As soon as we made the first incision its brain became fully aware, like it knew it was being cut open. But as it wasn't showing any physical reaction we continued with the dissection. With caution." She then looked to her assistants, inviting them to speak also.

Charles took over, "I started at the wound that you had caused in what would be the creatures neck. I could see that you had removed a large section of the spine -obviously what connected its mechanical limbs to its brain as there were rows of mechanic workings ending in broken shards close to the missing piece. But as I worked I could see that it was slowly regenerating. Rebuilding the missing part."

Charles paused for a moment to see if Kaia and Dean would have any questions, but they just sat there, ready to hear more. He cleared his throat and continued, "The pieces of metal that were still inside of it were whirring and clicking, changing to accommodate for the missing piece. Adapting to the injury. We believe this is why when you kill them, they don't stay dead for long."

Kaia and Dean nodded in understanding as fear and curiosity sank in. If they could adapt to any injury they received, they were essentially indestructible.

Janna spoke next, and they were surprised by her thick Scottish accent, "I was working on the creature's underbelly, and found that it had no organs." She noticed the looks of shock that came to Kaia and Dean's faces, and continued, "Yup. That's about how I looked too -with just a touch of intrigue. Anyways. Instead, there was just a large sphere that emitted more electricity than anything I've come across in my career. It could easily power the entire continent of North America and then some. I tried to remove it, but anytime anything would go near it, it would create a deadly spark. We just don't have the equipment to handle something that generates such a mass quantity of power. I do think though, that this power could be the key to the creature's undoing."

Janna's face opened up into a huge smile, a smile that contained knowledge and hope, and the Generals' physiques, that had begun to slump in their chairs, perked up again at the sight.

"It'll be dangerous, but I believe that if we can get the majority of them, if not all of them, into one area, we could perform an emp triangulation shutdown, and finally put an end to this."

Dean and Kaia's eyes widened as they thought about the logistics of what accomplishing that would entail.

Gi stepped up and spoke next, "I have complete faith myself and our tech crew can design such a device and it will work. It's up to you to organize the troops and design the battle plans though."

Kaia and Dean nodded at each other.

"Okay, so we've heard the bad news, and the good news. But what about this peculiar news?" Dean asked.

Seong spoke again, "Well, as we were dissecting I found something in its brain. A chip. I plugged the chip into our computer, and a list popped up."

"What kind of list?" Kaia asked, caution and fear filling her voice as she remembered the awful vision she had experienced just hours earlier.

"A list of names. We're not sure what it means, but both of your names are on that list."

"Was there anyone else?" Kaia asked.

"We stopped looking after we saw yours." Seong said, "Figured you'd want to see it for yourselves.

Dean and Kaia looked at each other, knowing they should talk in private before continuing the conversation.

"Thank you Dr. Lee. We'll be back to talk more later." Kaia said.

Chapter 4

The sunrise glittered through the small windows that ran across the wall at ceiling height as Kaia and Dean left The Lab and headed to the dining hall for breakfast.

"That list, it's got to have something to do with our ability." Kaia said quietly, "Maybe we should tell them about it."

Dean shook his head, "That's the exact reason why we left that place to begin with. So that we wouldn't be treated like rats in a maze anymore."

Kaia sighed, remembering the terrible facility they grew up in. The dark hallways, the terrible screams, the barred windows, the constant guard watch. It was a prison in every sense of the word, except they were no criminals.

"Yes, but it would be different this time. We would be in trusting hands, we would be in control. And they wouldn't be experimenting on us."

Dean stopped and pulled her to the side, out of the way of the slowly increasing number of people heading the same way they were.

"I can't let someone go into my head again. You're the only one."

"But-"

"I'm sorry Kaia. I just can't."

Kaia sighed and looked down, taking her husbands hands, "Why won't you tell me what they did to you there?"

"Because if I told you you'd run off on some suicide mission." He said, a touch of humor in his voice.

Kaia kissed him and tightened her hold on his hands.

"Can you do me a favor though?"

"Anything." Dean smiled.

"Will you at least think about it. I believe it would help. There's a reason for that list, and there's a reason we're on it. What if we're somehow connected to these creatures. It would explain why they target us so much more than the others, and even more so when we're together. I just... I'm going to do it, and I would love for you to be with me."

Kaia let go of his hands and continued down the hall, leaving Dean standing there.

By the time Dean joined his wife she had already almost finished her meal, and as he stood there looking down at her, he knew what he had to do. Dean pulled a chair out and sat down to the plate Kaia had brought for him then said, "You're right. There's definitely a reason as to why our names are on that list, and we need to figure that out. But I'm not letting you go in there alone." He flashed a smile, one that shone from his eyes as well.

Kaia looked up from where she had been pushing some fruit around on her plate, and her heart melted at the smile on Dean's face.

"Thank you. We should go back to Dr. Lee as soon as we're finished. The sooner we figure this all out the better."

Dean nodded, and they finished their breakfast quickly with fear and hope swirling in their heads at the possibilities of what they would discover.

Chapter 5

Before heading back to The Lab Kaia and Dean went to The Lobby, a sizeable room just before the door that leads to the entrance, to oversee the return of the night crew, and give the a.m battle order(B.O) to the day crew. As always they hoped they wouldn't have to make any obituaries, but they hadn't had a clean night in months.

"That's seventeen today. Just gone." Dean said with a hollow sadness in his voice.

"It's getting worse. We need this plan of Dr. Grey's to work."

Kaia's voice reflected the tone of Dean's, and he squeezed her shoulder compassionately.

She rested her hand on top of his and sighed, "Let's go then."

The whooshing of the heavy steel doors sliding open startled Seong, her sudden reaction knocking several items to the ground.

"I'm so sorry Dr. Lee. I didn't mean to startle you like that. Let me help."

Kaia rushed to Seong's side, helping to pick up the various items; among them many coffee cups.

"It's alright, I was really off in my own little world there." Seong said as she straightened up her work area, "What can I do for you?"

"We're here to check out that list of names you mentioned earlier." Dean said.

"Of course, this way."

The pair followed Seong over to a small computer in the corner of the room, and watched as she clicked through a series of icons. She stepped away, sliding the chair over to them, as a dark red window filled with names occupied the screen.

"There you go."

"Thank you." Kaia nodded at Seong.

"I'll just be over there if you need anything." Seong tucked a stray hair behind her ear, her bun looking even more disheveled than normal, and pointed to the table she was working at when they came in.

Dean sat down in the chair while Kaia briefly watched Seong walk back to her workstation; she looked like she could use a solid twenty-four hours of sleep. Kaia turned back to the small computer and leaned over the desk, one hand on Dean's shoulder.

As the list of names loaded it almost seemed like time was slowing down, and names began to blur into one another, as though something was trying to stop them from seeing them. They concentrated harder and eventually names began to stick out, like little highlighted sections in an ocean of incomprehensible babble. Every time they saw one it felt like little fireworks going off in their heads as flashes of memories passed by.

Jayde Traykler
Steven Rhee
Abe O'Connell
Demi Nuada
Chris Mikami
Natalee Ludoviko
Imogene Kaelin
Mark Harlin
Lauren Greene
Kurtis Gard
Thomas Dashner
Samantha Darkholme
Hannah Adler

The list kept going, but they had seen enough. Too many friends that were long gone, and too many painful memories bubbling to the surface. But there were two names that stood out the most.

We have to find Sam and Hannah.

Dean nodded in agreement.

Kaia clicked out of the list of names and turned off the monitor.

"Dr. Lee?" Kaia spoke softly.

Seong turned her head slowly, rubbing her eyes.

"We'll be in touch soon." She paused for a moment, then continued with, "You should really go get some rest."

"I will, I'm just finishing up my report on the dissection."

"Okay." Kaia smiled at her softly, then followed her husband out.

Dean and Kaia began their search for Sam and Hannah, scouring the base from top to bottom.

"I can't believe we didn't know they were there with us." Kaia said.

"It was a big place, and there were a lot of us. It is possible we just never ran into them." Dean replied.

After over an hour of searching it became obvious that Sam and Hannah were out in the field. Standing by the door that would lead them to the entrance Dean noticed Kaia had started biting her nails -which she only did when she was particularly anxious.

He took the hand that was by her mouth, and tilted her face up, "It'll be lunchtime in a couple of hours, and they might come back for rotation. We can wait by the entrance for them."

Kaia nodded, almost in a trance, "I wonder if any of those other people are here with us."

Her mind drifted back to one name in particular.

Chapter 6

"Do you love him?"

"Shutup Kaia! I mean... maybe. Oh, I don't know. We've only met once."

Kaia looked at her friend, a look that told her she knew that there was more to it than that.

"Okay, so we've only met," Lauren did the hand gesture for quotation marks as she said 'met', "the one time, but it's like we're with each other all the time. ...If that makes sense. Is this what it was like for you when you first met Dean?"

"Lights out!" A voice boomed from the hall, and the girls quickly got under their blankets just before their door opened. "I said-" The voice stopped and sighed, "God damned kids."

The light was flicked out, and the door came closed with a heavy metal scrape; an awful sound that the girls had grown used to. Kaia peeked out from under her blankets as the sound of footsteps disappeared, then hit the bottom of the bunk above her to let Lauren know the coast was clear. Lauren climbed down to the lower bunk, and got under the blanket with Kaia.

"When I first met Dean... Well, it was just different than meeting anyone else I'd ever met in my life. We had this unspoken... connection. It was special, it-"

"Allows you to talk to each other without being with each other?"

"How did you...?

"Steven and I can do the same thing!"

"Shh." Kaia clapped her hand down over Lauren's mouth.

Heavy footsteps could be heard approaching their door, and the girls held their breath at the expected appearance of a guard. But the steps continued past and down the hallway, and they let out a sigh of relief.

"Sorry." Lauren whispered.

"It's okay. I've got a year longer on this place than you do, and trust me, I don't plan on being here any longer than I have to."

Lauren saw a fire in her friend's eyes that she had never seen in anyone before, so she opted for not continuing that route of conversation.

"How long have you guys been here? You can't be much older than eighteen."

"I am. I was brought here when I was sixteen. Around the same time Dean showed up, so I'd seen him around, but we didn't meet until last year."

"When did you find out that you could... you know, talk to each other?"

"The night we met. Throughout the day I could tell something wasn't right, and when it came to lights out the feeling was so strong I couldn't sleep. Soon all I could hear were screams inside my head. It only took an hour or so to figure out it was him, but it felt like endless days worth of screaming. It was awful."

Lauren's eyes had gone wide listening to the story, and her voice reflected the horror she felt, "What did they do to him?"

"I don't know. He still won't tell me what they did to him that night."

"Can you talk to me?" Lauren asked the question, wanting to change the subject before the pain in her friend's eyes became the tears that were threatening them.

"What?"

"I mean, well... the way you and Dean do, the way Steven and I do. We must be able to talk to each other also."

"I never thought of that. I can't believe they never thought of that. What if they did. What if..." By the end Kaia was talking to herself.

Lauren was used to Kaia going off into her own little world as her train of thought took over, and ignored it.

"Why don't we try it?" Lauren smiled at Kaia and sat up on the bed.

Kaia stopped her mumbling and sat up too. Focusing on where her ability stemmed from, as opposed to who she wanted to talk to, she attempted to speak into Lauren's mind. Immediately Dean was in her mind's eye, and she smiled. Kaia forced Dean out of focus, not away, just out of the main focus. She dug deeper, searching for the source of the ability. There, tucked in between where the emotional meets the primal part of the brain. Kaia held onto that and turned her focus to Lauren. She never remembered communication being so hard with Dean, it just came naturally; after that first incident anyways.

Lauren.

Kaia looked up, and Lauren still had the same smile of ambition as before. She took a deep breath and tried again.

Lauren!

"Woah, not so loud." Lauren grabbed the left side of her head, right above her ear.

Without saying anything Kaia quickly grabbed Lauren's hand, and moved her hair out of the way. She found a tiny scar about the size of a freckle.

"What? What is it?" Lauren asked.

Kaia grabbed Lauren's finger and rubbed it against the scar.

"Do you feel that?"

"Feel what?" Lauren asked, her confusion evident in her eyes.

"Here, look. Do you see anything?"

Kaia turned her head to the side while tucking hair behind her left ear to reveal to Lauren what she knew was there.

"No, I don't see anything. What are you- ... Wait a second. Yeah, there's a tiny scar here. Wait, is that what you saw on me?" Lauren's hand crept back up to her head where her own scar was.

"Yes. It's got to be an implant of some kind. Microscopic, and clearly implanted by amazing doctors. It's got to be what gives us this... ability." Kaia was speaking to herself again. When she was finished rambling she blinked and looked back up at Lauren.

"We should get to sleep. We'll try to communicate with each other again some other time."

Kaia laid back down and rolled over, pulling the blanket up over her head. Lauren knew that Kaia needed to be alone with her thoughts now, and climbed back up to her own bunk.

Chapter 7

Rotation had come and gone, for the most part, but there was still no sign of Sam and Hannah -which was typical for them and the other squad leaders. Kaia had begrudgingly agreed that waiting would get them nowhere, so they went for lunch themselves.

Both had finished eating, and Dean could see the impatience and anxiety that waiting for Sam and Hannah's return was rising within Kaia: the tapping foot, the fingernail biting, the restless eyes, the rigid way she held her body.

Dean pushed his chair away from the table, stood up, and broke the tense silence. "Alright then, let's go."

"Thank you."

As the word came out of her mouth all of the tension left, her eyes lit up, her body visibly loosened, and her chair almost fell over in her haste to get up. Dean chuckled at the outburst then followed her out of the dining hall.

After gearing up they approached the main doors of the base and saw that Ben and Freddie were still standing at guard duty -which only meant one thing. Their rotation never came back. They were dead.

"Ben, Freddie." Dean and Kaia acknowledged the pair as they opened the doors for them; the shared knowledge of mourning the evident loss of life reflected in their faces.

They stepped outside and the doors shut behind them creating a waft of air that sent shivers up and down their bodies. The smell hit them first. Always the same putrid smell the creatures emanated -like diesel mixed with burnt hair and festering wounds. That mingled with the coppery smell of blood created an invisible cloud that always assaulted the senses immediately. No matter how much time you spent in it.

"Did I ever tell you that I threw up the first time that smell hit me?" Kaia said, staring out at the wasteland.

"Only a couple." Dean chuckled and looked over at his wife; she was practically glowing.

There was an excitement bubbling up between the two that hadn't been there in a long time. Mr. and Mrs. Whittaker were on the battlefield together once more.

They eventually came upon twelve of their comrades up against three of the creatures, and quickly ducked behind a large uprooted tree. The tree corpse was jutting up out of the ground at an awkward angle, and some of the larger roots that were exposed had created a basket-like cover. Hiding behind it made them effectively out of view, but still allowed them to see what was happening.

While looking out at the battle they noticed that all five Colonels were present: Jack Fisher, Amara Juana, Sasha Ayers, Gerard Barker, and Ki Cho Hyeong. Fighting alongside them were a few remaining soldiers -Ryan, Lily, David, and two unknowns- but mostly it was a field of dead bodies strewn about like ragdolls.

Something bad must have happened to have all them all here together.

Dean knew Kaia was referring to the five Colonels who typically remained separated with their own squads.

Who are they? Kaia asked as she pointed to one of the unknowns.

It was a woman whose face was covered by the shadow of a hood, and carried a large sniper rifle on her back. She dodged a strike from one of the creatures, then fired several shots into where the attacking limb met its body with dual pistols.

No idea, but look. There!

Dean pointed, and they watched as Sam and Hannah rolled out from behind, and fired at, the same creature the unknown woman was battling against.

Suddenly there was an intense heat, an awful smell, and a gurgling sound right behind them. Kaia and Dean held their breath as they looked behind themselves to see the blood-spattered face of one of the creatures. It was so close they could taste its hot breath on their faces. It hiccuped, and a bubble of blood popped between its teeth; strips of flesh from a previous kill still dangling from them.

"Run!" Dean yelled as he threw his fist into one of the creature's eyes. A high-pitched screech emitted from the creature, and Kaia sprinted away, confident Dean was right behind her.

But he wasn't.

Dean's fist had gone right through the eye socket and into the muscle of its face. He was elbow deep in the squishy flesh, and it was contracting around him, trapping him as it retreated. Its limbs crashed into each other, and Dean was tossed around like a ragdoll in the creature's effort to try and escape. He tried to pull his arm free, but it was hopeless. Dean was being dragged away.

Kaia reached the creature that Sam, Hannah, and the unknown woman was facing first. Just as Kaia was directly behind the creature she dropped to her knees and slid underneath it, dragging a knife across its underbelly. The gray slime-blood poured down on her as she slid through, and Kaia could see the brightness of the electric sphere Janna had talked about. As Kaia emerged on the other side, slime-blood dripping from her arms, the three women looked at her with surprise in their eyes. The creature screeched and wailed as it spasmed, trying desperately to hold its underbelly together. The four women aimed their weapons and fired until it stopped moving.

Kaia looked for it, but the brightness of the power sphere was barely visible through the torn flesh and blood. She stepped towards it, wanting to get a better look when a voice tore through her mind.

Kaia!

Kaia's head whipped in the direction that her husband's voice was coming from.

"You three go help the others. I'll be back." Kaia said, but as she turned to run a hand grabbed her arm.

"Wait, I'm coming with you."

Kaia could see Sam and Hannah running towards the others. It was the strange woman, her face still shadowed by the large hood. Kaia didn't have time to question her, so she just nodded and ran.

It didn't take long before Kaia could see Dean trapped within the panicked creature. Their eyes met just as it turned and started making another attempt to escape from the pain in its eye. Kaia sprinted even harder, all of her focus bent on reaching Dean before it was too late. She didn't even notice the strange woman disappear.

Kaia pulled an Ithaca 37 out of the holster on her back, and fired off three rounds as she sprinted; they all missed. She redoubled her efforts on getting closer to the creature, and a sharp pain began to seer through her lungs. Kaia ignored the pain and ran on, determination blaring from her eyes.

Dean struggled against the pressure that was wrapped around his arm. He kicked at the creature, trying to knock the limbs out from under it as they passed by him but it was useless. Suddenly there was a loud bang, and the creature stumbled, alleviating the pressure on Dean's arm. Dean kicked backward off of the creature and, just before he would have been crushed by its falling body, chaotically rolled across the ground. Before he had a chance to stand up Kaia was practically on top of him, unshed tears shining in her eyes.

Dean held her face, "It's okay. I'm okay." He smiled, but she didn't look reassured.

"What's wrong?"

"It wasn't me."

"What do you mean?"

"I didn't shoot it." Kaia revealed a bullet scratch on the side of her forearm, "I don't know if they were trying to get me, or you, or the creature," She was starting to ramble, "I don't even know where it came from."

"It was me."

Dean and Kaia looked towards the source of the voice to see the unknown woman standing there, with what they could see now was an XM2010 sniper. It was almost as long as she was tall.

"And I was definitely aiming for the creature."

She pulled the large hood down away from her face to reveal medium length brown hair, beautiful green eyes, and a petite face frame to match her lithe body.

Kaia stared at her, raw emotions displayed on her face. She stood up and tripped a little on Dean's foot as she walked towards the woman.

"...Lau-Lauren?"

The woman nodded, her smile broadening, and tears forming in her eyes.

"I can't believe you're here!" Kaia embraced Lauren, and the two women laughed and cried at their reunion.

When they finally pulled back from each other Dean was standing beside them, stretching out his injured arm.

"I've heard a lot about you." Dean said, offering a hand to shake Lauren's.

"Likewise. Well, up until you two left. What happened?"

"We have a lot to talk about, but first we need to go back to the others, make sure they're okay. Then we can get back home and talk." Kaia said.

"Watch out!"

Sam pushed Hannah just before one of the creature's limbs would have speared right through her. Sam fired her machine gun mercilessly into the creature's face, screaming, until there was nothing left but a black goopy mess. Somehow the thing still managed to screech out a blood-curdling sound that made the hair stand up on the back of her neck.

Ryan ran up from behind the creature, jumped onto its back, and, as he landed, drove the bayonet of his rifle into its neck. The creature shook Ryan from its back, the bayonet breaking off, sending him and the rifle tumbling to the ground. Sparks and smoke emerged from where the weapon was embedded in its neck.

"Aw man." Ryan muttered to himself as he saw the broken nub at the end of his rifle.

The creature tried to move towards the group to continue the attack, but its limbs stuttered and popped until it tripped over itself and fell to the ground. Ryan rolled out of the way with seconds to spare, and when he looked up he saw Sam's hand reaching down to help him up.

"Thanks."

"Ditto." She said.

The three ran towards the rest of their group to help take down the last creature.

Dean, Kaia, and Lauren came running into the battle just in time to see Ki get trapped under one of the creatures. The three of them sprinted towards the scene, and as they did Dean pulled on an armoured glove; something he'd wished he'd had time to do earlier.

As Ki lay pinned under the sharp end of one of the creature's limbs, the only thing stopping him from being skewered, and just barely at that, was the handle of his MP5.

"Guys!" He shouted, "I don't know how much longer I got here!"

Holding the gun in place was taking an effort that wouldn't last much longer, and though the others were trying to distract it, to pull it away and off of Ki, it wouldn't take the bait. Dean was only a couple of feet away when the steepness of the hill caught up to him and he careened downwards, tripping over his feet as he tumbled towards Ki. In the last second he managed to gain control of his body, and threw his fist into the creature's limb, knocking Ki free of its death grip. Following the momentum of the punch Dean went flying over Ki's body, then rolled to a stop just short of where the creature stumbled away, tripping over its own limbs.

Ki was dusting himself off as Dean turned around.

"Thanks man." Ki said, his eyes still wide with fear.

"Don't mention it." Dean said, and they joined firing at the creature with the others.

Lauren had set up her sniper at the top of the hill, and was peering down the scope, waiting for an opening. Kaia stayed with her in case anything else showed up, but that didn't stop her from firing as many rounds into the creature below them as she could.

Finally, Lauren's opening was available. Just as the creature was about to come crushing down for the kill on the group below she fired, and it hit directly into that section of the spine where it meets the neck; the same spot that Ryan's bayonet was lodged in the other one. The creature immediately ceased all cognitive movement and began to fall. Dean and the others ran out of the way of the landing zone just in time to get hit with a cloud of dust.

Lauren and Kaia regrouped just as the coughs and splutters were dying down. Kaia approached Sam and Hannah, ready to tell them she had information they needed to know, when suddenly the ground began to shake. They all looked to the top of the hill the women had just come from to see seven more of the creatures emerge from the tree line.

"Run! Now!" Kaia yelled.

The group ran faster and harder than they'd ever run before, desperate to reach the safety of the base. It was suicide to look back, so when that scream was heard -that scream that signified someone had been caught up to and killed- they could only run harder.

They ran around trees and rocks, jumped over roots and cracks in the ground, dodged and rolled whenever one of the creature's limbs got too close, and fired behind them as often as they could. Finally the base was visible, a glowing beacon of hope in the distance, and the sight of home instilled hope into those remaining.

Freddie could feel the ground vibrating beneath his feet, and he turned to look through a tube that led up and out of the ceiling -The Pipe. He could see his comrades running for their lives, a billowing cloud of dust, and several creatures fast approaching. As the sight greeted him he could only watch as Lily was snatched from the ground, tossed into the air, and ripped apart.

"Ben! The doors! Now!"

Ben flipped a switch, and the release of a puff of air could be heard as the locks disengaged. The two Captains raised their weapons, ready to fire at the creatures, but the dust cloud was too thick, and the risk of hitting one of their own too great. Ben let his hand hover over the switch, ready to flip it the second everyone was inside.

With a final push of adrenaline those remaining reached the doors and dove through with seconds to spare. The boom of the creatures colliding with the doors shuddered through the floor and walls. They all sat, or stood, and listened with weapons aimed at the doors. As the sound of the creatures faded into the distance they finally dropped their weapons, and let the weariness in their bodies take over. Dean slumped down against the wall, leaning his head back and resting his sore arm on one raised knee. Kaia chose to stay standing and leaned against the wall beside him with her arms hanging by her side.

Ben was about to speak when he saw the look of bitter hatred that clung to Sasha's face. He quickly sidestepped out of the way and watched as the Colonel continued her way down the hall.

"This is such bullshit. We just keep dying out there." Sasha voiced what everyone else was thinking as she stormed away, shoving a Goncz pistol back into her holster. Gerard caught up to her and wrapped an arm around her shoulders, stopping her, just as the doors whooshed behind them.

"No one else would be able to get that close to her right now." Jack said. Although there was an edge of humor to his voice, the inevitable weariness of the whole situation was evident in his face.

"What even happened out there?" Kaia asked, still resting against the wall.

"It's like we all got ambushed out there at once. They were acting like more of an army than the isolated attacks we're used to, and it wasn't long before we all got pushed together. It was a massacre, and I'm sure if you two hadn't have shown up when you did none of us would have made it."

"How many did we lose?" Kaia asked with a hollowness to her voice.

"At least fifty." Jack ran a hand through his hair and sighed, "I don't know how much longer we have." And with that he took his leave, Ki and Amara following close behind.

Kaia and Dean shared a look, one that said the words their minds didn't need to. We **need** this plan to work. Kaia pushed herself off the wall and looked down to where Sam and Hannah had slid to the floor.

"Sam, Hannah, we need to talk. Meet us in the dining hall in two hours." As Kaia spoke she pulled off her slime-blood covered tactical jacket, and it made a 'slop' sound as she let the material fall together at her side.

Sam and Hannah made no response, just sat there looking dumbfounded staring at the ground. "Sam? Hannah?" Kaia walked over to them, "Are you okay?"

Hannah looked up, "Huh, what-oh. Yeah, sorry. It's just..."

Sam picked up on the train of thought, "If it weren't for Ryan we'd be dead. And now he's gone. And David, and Lily, and countless others. It's just... I'm so sick of this war."

Kaia nodded solemnly, no words were needed to know that everyone felt the same way. The girls sighed and agreed to meet later, then pulled themselves up off the ground and left.

Dean finally stood up, and the Generals left with Lauren and the unknown man, leaving Ben and Freddie behind at their post. They headed to the equipment room to return their gear, bringing the two newcomers with them.

Kaia kept glancing over at the unknown man as they made their way, she had a suspicion of who he was. His appearance was that of Asian-American descent, with short but shaggy black hair, chocolate brown eyes, and the type of muscular build you get from simply surviving.

"Steven, I'm guessing?" Kaia asked, offering her hand to shake.

“The one and only.” He replied.

“You two better come with us when we talk to Sam and Hannah. But first showers and fresh clothes.” Kaia said, a half disgusted look on her face as she carefully picked up her soiled jacket.

Chapter 8

Dean and Kaia arrived shortly after the others had started digging into large dinners. With only a few bites left on each plate, Kaia began the conversation with one thought on the forefront of her mind.

Why can't I remember seeing them there?

"Well, I guess some introductions are in order. Sam and Hannah, meet Lauren and Steven. They uh... they escaped from Grady too." Kaia said referring to herself and Dean, but she watched to see if any kind of recognition crossed Sam and Hannah's faces. It didn't. Just the usual look of disgust and disbelief someone has when Grady's name is mentioned.

"Lauren, why don't you tell us how you two got here." Kaia passed the attention over to Lauren, who faltered for a second before beginning their story.

"Well, it didn't take long after you two left before everything started falling apart. There was a steady incline of panic among the Authorities when they realized that two more had escaped, let alone you two. Classes, " Lauren did the hand gesture for quotation marks as she said 'classes', "started getting cancelled. We were locked in our rooms for the majority of the time. Then one day they came to Steven and brought him to an observatory of sorts. Grady has cameras everywhere. He's spreading out. Rebuilding cities. Rebuilding the world according to his rule. He has his Authorities guarding the places like some sort of prison camps."

Steven took over at this point, "He claims he's saving them. Lost survivors, looking for stability. People get sick, they need doctors. They need doctors, they need society. And he was offering structured villages. Probably the only close-to-a-good-thing he'll ever do with his repertoire. Went and ruined it with the prison camp theme. Anyways. They pulled me, and a few others, for observation duty. To try and find you. But as we had to start looking further out, they pulled us off the job. Probably realized we'd get too good of an idea of what's out there, and he'd have more escapes on his hands. Asshole. Lucky for us, I did figure a way out, and I figured out about this place. Not through the cameras, he hasn't spread that far yet. I found out about this place when digging around in their files while they weren't looking. Not so lucky for us, I got caught snooping around looking for more information. Something we could bring with us to help launch an attack." Steven paused for a moment, reorganizing his thoughts before he continued with what he'd found. "The little of what I managed to discover was that they had drifted away from trying to find you two, and had begun working on a plan B, so to speak. Something about activating a memory swipe in the chips they'd put in us, and that there had been successful trials of it. But the results also included losing everything Grady had done to us. And he didn't want that, so he refused to let it happen again. Sick bastard. Anyways, I wasn't having any luck trying to find blueprints of the place, so I started making my own." Steven pulled out a handful of messily sketched maps from a knapsack as he spoke, "I would sneak out at night and explore the vents, drawing maps of them. Eventually I stumbled on a section of the facility I couldn't reach using the vents. I'd mapped the entire inner workings and had yet to find the hidden space. So it had to be only accessible from outside. I found it." There was something hollow about the way he said that last part. Steven paused again, sighing and shaking his head. Looking down at the table he closed his eyes and a took a deep breath in, as if reliving what he saw as he spoke. "What I found was madness. Just the freakiest shit I'd ever seen. Creatures so twisted and dark they practically manifested darkness itself. Oversized lanky things with thick leathery skin that resembled people, but definitely weren't. Faceless monsters with weaponized limbs."

A shiver ran down Steven's spine, and Lauren took over again.

"That night Steven never came back. I knew what his plan was, and I knew that it was riskier than his usual outings, that it would take longer. But eventually I couldn't wait anymore. I tried to reach out to him, but I didn't get any kind of response."

No one noticed the look that came across Sam and Hannah's faces at this point. It was as though someone had stolen their breath and their hearts skipped a beat all at once.

"I immediately started poking around trying to find him. It took weeks, and a lot of pretending around the Authorities on my part, but eventually I found him. Unfortunately, I wound up in the same position as him. They kept us drugged the whole time, and if we hadn't have gotten out when we did I'm willing to bet we would have become one of those monsters Steven stumbled on."

Kaia sensed the anxiety rising in her husband and squeezed his thigh, bringing him back down to earth. He took her hand and squeezed back, grateful for her ability to to keep him grounded when those memories came creeping back, threatening to overwhelm him. He loved her so much in that moment for that.

"How did you get out?" Kaia asked.

"Pure dumb luck." Lauren said, a small smile on her face as she ran a hand through her hair. "Just over a month ago, in the middle of the night, there was a tremor that shook through the facility. It knocked Steven loose of the machine that was holding him down. He disconnected me from mine, and we grabbed as much data and weaponry as we could before hightailing it out of there. We hijacked one of their helicopters and flew it a months trek away from here. Near one of the old cities he hasn't stretched out to yet to throw them off."

"Looks more like a shanty town now." Steven added.

Just as Lauren was about to continue Sam spoke, and for the first time the group noticed the expressions Sam and Hannah wore in reaction to hearing Lauren and Steven's story. "Hannah and I haven't *spoken* to each other since...well I can't remember how long. I asked her about it one day only to come to the conclusion that it was something I had dreamed. But it wasn't a dream...?" There was something hopeless about the way she whispered that last part. Like something inside her had broken.

Kaia had been waiting for some kind of recognition from the women, and this was the closest thing to it, so she figured now was as good a time as any to mention the list. Looking into Sam's eyes she said, "Do you remember that creature Dean brought back with him? The one I got you to take to Dr. Lee?"

Sam nodded.

"Well she extracted a microchip from it, and on it was a list. A list of names. Including mine and Dean's, and Lauren's and Steven's... and yours and Hannah's."

Sam's eyes were bright with the unshed tears she was fighting so hard to keep back.

"You two must have been at the facility at some point. Can you remember being there at all?"

Sam could only shake her head slowly from side to side, her hands trembling.

"They must have been the swipe trials I'd heard of." Steven said, his voice rising up out of the tension in the air like a charmed cobra. Steven's gaze landed on the two women, and his heart ached at the pain he saw etched into their faces. "When he saw his work in them was gone he must have let them go to wander free. Survive on their own somehow." It was a cruel statement, and he said it with as much softness as he could muster, but it was one that was true to who Grady was.

"We wandered around for weeks... months. Going from crummy town to crummier town. Barely surviving. Running from scavengers and madmen gone crazy from loneliness. And the cannibals... Until we came here." Hannah's voice held such raw emotion as she spoke of the types of people they'd run into it almost broke Kaia's heart, and it made her hate Grady even more. If that was possible.

"So not only did the awful things that we heard about what Grady does happen to us, but he sent us to that kind of a fate. Dumping us out like yesterday's garbage." Sam said, anger building in her voice, and her fists balling up as she spoke.

Hannah's eyes reflected the same pain in Sam's voice, and she reached a hand over to Sam, gently placing it over her shaking wrist. Kaia watched the subtle interaction, could see how they anchored each other, and it touched her heart in a way nothing else could in moment.

"We need to get to Dr. Lee. Kaia said, breaking the tension in the air, "Have her and her team remove the chips from us."

Dean and Kaia shared a quick look; the thought of losing their special form of communication was almost unbearable. It was so much a part of their life, they felt like a part of their intimacy was dying. Kaia caught the same look shared between Lauren and Steven, and her heart dropped another notch.

"As much as Steven says Grady won't risk losing his work," Kaia hated the words as they came out of her mouth, "I don't want to risk getting swiped. Besides, maybe they'll provide some useful information, because there's no way those creatures out there aren't connected to all of this. Chips in our heads, chips in theirs. If Grady had his way he'd have the whole damn world chipped, all bending to his every whim." Kaia took a breath to calm herself, then gestured to Lauren and Steven finishing with, "We'll give her all the stuff you brought with you as well."

Sam absent-mindedly rubbed at the tiny scar that had always been just behind her left ear. "Would removing it help us remember? I mean, I know what happened, because you said it. But I don't remember it. It's so... unsettling."

"There's no way to know that for sure, but it would be best to have it removed either way. We'll meet at The Lab in the morning after the a.m-B.O."

Sam nodded. The reality of what was happening -had happened- still had her, and Hannah, in a state of shock.

Chapter 9

As Kaia slept she dreamt of her vision again, and the scene before her was horrific. The entrance to the base was destroyed, and the doors had been ripped away, leaving wires to swing into each other, sending sparks flying. Lights dangled from the ceiling, flickering when they swung too far away from their power source. But the destruction of the building paled in comparison to the destruction of life that covered it. There was blood everywhere, and bodies were strewn across the place, groaning and crying, pleading for death to hurry and claim them. It was a massacre. Nobody seemed to notice her as she walked by; she was as a ghost to them. Then she found them.

Dean, impaled on one of the creature's sharpened limbs. Blood dripping from his mouth. Freddie, pinned against a broken wall, guts spilling out of his abdomen tumbling to the ground; a great shadow stepping over him. Electricity sparking. Hannah, eyes wide open but glazed over with death, bloody and limp. Sam, shirt ripped open, covered in blood, her remaining arm stretched out towards Hannah, blood gurgling out of her mouth as she sputtered her last breaths. Ben, legs gone, screaming; the shadow getting closer. Dean, reaching out for her. So much blood.

Kaia's eyes flew open, she was sweating and breathing heavily. She looked to where her husband should be and panicked. He was gone. The confusion and horror of the vision had left her incapable of coherent thought. She swung her legs over the side of the bed and sat holding her head in her hands, trying to force the panic out and think rationally. Somewhere in the distance of her mind the sound of rushing water could be heard. She was spiraling out of control and everything was going fuzzy. Suddenly a hand grabbed her shoulder, and she spun around, pure terror etched into her face.

"Is everything okay?" Dean asked.

Kaia, tears glistening in her eyes, didn't say anything. She simply fell into Dean's body and sobbed. He wrapped his arms around her and pulled her into the comfort of the bed.

Dean kissed her forehead and stroked her hair, wondering what could have possibly caused such a reaction in her. He had never seen such a look of fear come across her face before, no matter how bad it got in Grady's facility.

When the sounds of Kaia's light snoring replaced her sobbing Dean gently wiped the tear-tracks away, pulled her closer, and let himself drift off with her.

The rest of the night went uninterrupted.

Chapter 10

Sam and the others had gathered in the hallway outside The Lab to wait for Dean and Kaia. There wasn't a point to joining the B.O meeting as they weren't going out, so they had taken the opportunity to sleep in for once. But as the clock ticked on, and Dean and Kaia were nowhere to be seen, they grew worried.

Lauren spoke, an attempt to break the silence, and ease the tension that was growing among them.

"So you said you guys ran into cannibals out there?"

Hannah, who had taken to squatting against the wall, glanced up at Sam -she had begun pacing- before responding.

"Yeah. When he sent us out there, there were no cameras. No structured towns. He hadn't started that project yet I guess. It was just makeshift shanty towns that a few people had thrown together, scorched earth, and lost survivors making do with what they could. Some were so scared they wouldn't even approach us, and on the other end of the spectrum, there were others ready to tear us limb from limb just to get a scrap of anything to eat. There was this boy..."

Sam turned around in her pacing, and she locked eyes with Hannah. The threat of tears began to well up in both of their eyes as they remembered. Sam returned to her pacing, and Hannah continued with her story.

"He looked about seven years old. Skinniest thing I'd ever seen. And feral. The look in his eyes... it was terrifying and sad at the same time. It was like something out of a horror movie. Sam and I were on the brink of starving to death ourselves, and we'd only been out there for a month. This was his way of life, how he'd been raised. He came crawling towards us, his limbs all twitchy as he moved. Then he let out this shriek, and his mama came sprinting up over the hill. This crazed dash of madness, hair all matted and frizzed out from the elements, clothes ripped to shreds. ...I shot her, and she went tumbling down the hill, crashing into the poor boy. We didn't know what to expect at first, but of all the options running through our heads, what did happen was not one of them. He crawled over to her and... jammed his finger into the bullet hole. He knew she was dead. And then he just started eating her, jamming his fingers into the wound until it opened up more and more. He was tearing into her like some wild animal. I knew what had to be done, we both did. I couldn't bring myself to.... Sam did it."

Lauren and Steven glanced at Sam, but her back was to them.

"We buried them together. If there is an afterlife, I hope they found peace there."

Lauren was speechless, all she could think of to say was, "I'm so sorry."

Hannah stood back up and brushed away the tears that had fallen, "I just can't wait to get the chance to end that bastard's life. I mean, I know it's not his fault, that that's what became of that boy and his mother. That was just the result of the flare disaster, but a hell of a lot of other shit is, and he's gonna pay for that."

Sam's pacing finally paid off. When she turned around for the umpteenth time she was the first one to see Kaia and Dean come around the corner, each carrying a wounded soldier. She immediately sprang into action, running down the hallway to help.

"What happened?" Sam asked, taking some of the weight of the man Kaia was carrying.

"I don't know, they just collapsed as soon as they came in." Kaia responded.

The doors to The Lab opened, and Seong was sitting at a desk nearby. She was greeted with the sight of Dean,

Kaia, Sam, and Hannah carrying a couple of wounded soldiers.

"Hurry. Bring them this way." She said, jumping up and leading them through a smaller set of doors that opened up to a room where the walls were lined with cots and life-saving equipment -several people lay in some of the beds recuperating from injuries.

The four of them laid the men on a couple of beds on the far side of the room -away from the sleeping patients- while Seong hooked them up to the monitors.

Kaia stood beside her and spoke quietly, "Can you call the other doctors to duty for these men. I need the confidentiality of your team for what I'm about to tell you."

Seong nodded, and while continuing with what she was doing radioed for the other doctors to come at once. They arrived almost immediately and began working on the injured men. As Kaia left the room the men's shirts were cut open, and she could see serious bruising covering their bodies.

Janna and Charles, along with Steven and Lauren, were back in the other room waiting for them; Gi was busy working with the tech crew. Everyone sat down, or leaned against desks, and Kaia told the doctors the untold story of their time as Grady's subjects.

She told them of the facility they lived their teenage years in, of the true brutality of it. Of the physical training, the 'classes', the endless brain experiments, the chip implants, and their unique ability. Lauren took over at that point and told them of herself and Steven and how they fit into it all, what they went through, and how Sam and Hannah had experienced a memory swipe.

Before any questions could be asked Kaia opened the knapsack Lauren and Steven had brought with them, and handed the contents over to Seong. Her once tidy desk was now covered with various papers and data sticks. Seong picked up a couple pages and flipped through them, using the action as a way to go over everything in her head before speaking more than anything else.

"We'll get to work on this immediately. I'm sure these data sticks will be encrypted so it may take some time, but we'll do it."

"There is one other thing though." Kaia said.

"What's that?"

"We would like you to remove the chips they implanted in us. They may prove to be useful, or give some more insight to the situation. But more importantly, we don't want them in our heads."

Seong nodded. "Charles, Janna. Prep a private room with six beds please."

As everyone lay in their beds, anesthesia quickly kicking in, they watched the doctors move around the room until everything faded away. Deep inside Dean's anesthetic-induced sleep he drifted to an old memory.

He looked back over his shoulder at her as they were escorted back to their rooms; it was like the hole that had always been in his life was suddenly filled. It was a strange connection that fascinated and thrilled him, and he wanted nothing more than to see her again. A rough hand pushed on his shoulder, and he bit his tongue in an attempt to contain his anger as he tripped over his own feet from the force.

"Go on." The rough hand gestured into his room.

Dean walked in, stopping just short of the doorway.

"He's not going to be happy with you."

And with that the door slammed shut, almost hitting him. Dean stumbled forwards muttering to himself; he was sick of the mind games, sick of being treated like a child and a prisoner, sick of it all. He was ready to leave, but now that he had met her he couldn't leave her behind. Dean knelt down in front of his bed and sighed, reaching under the supporting planks where he kept-

"Looking for something?" A gruff voice, with the thickest Southern accent he'd ever heard, came from behind him.

Dean turned his head to see a man standing over him. He was at least seven feet tall, with a heavy build and thick combed back hair. He was sporting army green cargo pants with a black button-down shirt, had a toothpick sticking out of the corner of his mouth -a truly burly looking Southern man if he'd ever seen one- and was holding Dean's knapsack out.

Dean looked back to the ground for a moment and sighed before standing up to face the man. Being tall for his age, combined with the intense physical training he received at the facility, meant he didn't look quite as small as he could have in comparison, but this edge only increased his cockiness.

"And who are you?"

"I'm the reason why you're all here. I'm the one who calls the shots, and I'm the one who decides what happens to you after we find out what's in this bag."

Dean looked into the man's eyes, unflinching, as each item fell out of his upturned knapsack. A map, a few flares, some nonperishables, a couple of grenades, a gun, and some extra bullets.

"Well, well, well. Looks like we have an escape attempt on our hands." The man spat into the pile of items, somehow still keeping the toothpick in his mouth, then whistled sharply. Immediately five men and women fully decked out with weapons and riot gear burst in and escorted Dean out of his room. He was pulled through corridors and elevators until eventually they came to a dark chamber with a single chair in the center of it. Dean struggled and shouted as they strapped him to the chair, and as they left all he could do was stare at their backs helplessly.

Dean had begun to sweat in his sleep, and his eyelids fluttered and fingers twitched sporadically. Charles quickly scrawled some notes on a pad based on the monitor readings, then called Seong over with evident concern in his voice.

"Dr. Lee."

She came over quickly, leaving Sam and Hannah with Janna for a moment.

"He's not reacting as well to the procedure as the others are. It's not just the physical stuff; it's his heart rate. Every centimeter closer we get to chip it increases, then there's his breathing..."

Seong listened to Charles while looking over the monitors herself. The readings were unsettling, but still within reasonable expectation of the potential reactions to such a procedure. Especially considering the fact that they were working without the original tools that inserted them in the first place. It was mostly concerning because he was the only one out of the group reacting in such a way.

"Keep going. Just slow the extraction prong down a bit, and keep close watch over him. I'll finish up with Kaia."

Charles nodded and kept working.

Dean's vision wavered, and his throat was raw from shouting. The room seemed to spin around him, and the darkness coupled with the humidity threatened to overwhelm him. But just before he could pass out, the shock of pain came.

Over and over and over.

"Pl-...ple.." Dean mumbled, trying to get him to stop, but could barely get one word out.

"I'm sorry. I-I didn't quite catch that."

Somewhere in the murkiness of it all Dean heard him chuckle.

"St-" Dean was cut off as another shock went through him. His back arched up out of the chair, and the straps cut into the skin of his arms and legs as he threw his head back, screaming from the agony coursing through his body.

"Stooooooooop!"

Dean's body fell back into the chair, almost lifeless. He barely heard the footsteps echo towards him, and hardly felt the hand that slapped his face. He just wished the blackness that swam before his eyes would claim him and take him away. The hand grabbed his face, holding his head up, and Dean's eyelids fluttered in response.

"There won't be anymore escape attempts out of you, will there boy?"

Dean just sat there, unable to make his mouth form words.

"Shake your head for no."

Dean complied, and pain bounced off the walls of his skull. The Southern man let go of Dean's face, simultaneously pushing it. Dean lifted his head enough to see, through blurred vision, the man heading for the door.

"Oh, and one more thing." The Southern man walked back to where Dean sat and swung his fist hard into Dean's jaw. Dean knew he would have gone sprawling across the ground if it weren't for the chair he was strapped to, and the last words he heard before the darkness finally claimed him were, "I own you boy. You and everyone else here. Don't forget that."

And with that, it started all over again.

Chapter 11

Kaia paced back and forth as her husband was put, unconscious, into the CT Scanner the third time since she, and the others, had awoken from the procedure. The anesthesia had long worn off, and though they tried everything they knew, nothing would bring him out of his apparent coma. Kaia was biting at her nails, and she jumped a little when Seong came up from behind and tapped her on the shoulder.

"I think we should switch our focus to the information Lauren and Steven brought in. He's stable, and maybe if we find out more about your abilities, you'll be able to help in a way that we can't."

To Kaia's surprise, when they woke up, they all still had the innate ability to communicate within each other's minds, and Sam and Hannah regained theirs. Not only that, but it was also easier now, much easier. Kaia nodded, and realizing what she was doing shoved her hands into her pockets.

"You're right. How are the others?"

"Steven and Lauren are fine. They are still experiencing headaches, just as Sam and Hannah are. Just as you are." Seong's voice softened at that last part, and Kaia rubbed at her head.

"You need to get some rest."

Kaia almost responded with no, just as she had over the past near forty-eight hours, but she knew better, and nodded with a sigh.

"But come get me as soon as anything happens. I mean it."

"Of course."

Kaia left the antechamber her husband was in, leaving him with Seong, and looked at the large doors that led from the main area of The Lab back out to the hallway. She should have kept walking, but Kaia felt she had a duty to check in on the others first, including the two injured men herself and Dean had brought in earlier. She entered the ward the men were in and, carefully walking past the other sleeping patients, approached Dr. Grey who was seated beside them.

"Good to see you, Mrs. Whittaker. How are you feeling?" Dr. Grey greeted her. Her thick Scottish accent still sounded surprising as the first words came from her mouth.

"I am well enough, thank you. How are they doing?"

"They'll be fine. They'll be sore as hell for a while, but they'll live."

"What are their names?"

"Kurtis Gard, and Chris Mikami; soldiers under Colonel Jack Fisher."

A pang of recognition hit her, but she couldn't quite place it.

"Kurtis and Chris..." Kaia said the names out loud, speaking to herself more than Janna.

Janna watched the look of confused recognition play across Kaia's face as she walked around their beds, and as Kaia walked past Chris' head she bent down, looking closely behind his left ear.

"Is everything okay?" Janna stood up to try and see for herself what Kaia was taken aback by. "Mrs. Whittaker?" Janna asked, caution in her voice.

Without responding Kaia moved over to Kurtis. She moved his hair out of the way to look closely behind his left ear also.

"Kaia." Janna's voice was slightly louder this time, and Kaia looked up, the confusion gone from her face.

"These men have the same chips you just removed from us."

"What? How do you-"

"They have the same scars."

There was a pause, and Kaia looked between the two men, then up to Dr. Grey.

"Remove them."

"Shouldn't we wait until they're awake. Talk to them?"

"Remove them. Now." And with that Kaia walked out of the room, leaving Dr. Grey to begin the removal process again.

Kaia's next visit found her before she found it. As she turned the corner leading to the barracks hall she came across Lauren heading back to her new room.

"Hey. How are you and Steven?"

"We're fine. The headaches are almost gone, which is good. Is Dean still...?"

"Yes, but he's stable. I'm just checking on everyone before I get some rest myself."

"Good, you look like you need it." Lauren smiled.

Kaia let out a short chuckle, running a hand through her hair, and rubbing the back of her neck. "I don't doubt it."

Lauren's eyes softened, and she gave into the urge to hug her friend, "I've missed you."

"Same, and when all this over we'll find somewhere nice to relax with some wine and catch up. " She said, holding on the hug. Then pulling back, "I'll make sure to find better stuff than the crap I stole from Grady's stores that one night."

"Okay good, 'cause that stuff was awful." Lauren said, and the women laughed, remembering how they were almost caught with the stolen alcohol.

"I'm glad you're here." Kaia smiled softly, then wavered a little.

Lauren reached out quickly, grabbing her friends arm, stabilizing her. "Do you want me to walk you to your room?"

"No no, I'll be okay." Kaia stepped back, straightening herself out, "I'll see you at breakfast tomorrow."

Kaia waved as she walked away, then headed for her next stop, Sam and Hannah. She could hear the girl's voices as she approached their room.

Knock. Knock. Knock.

"Come in." Sam said, opening the door with a wide smile on her face.

"Glad to see you're doing well." Kaia said, walking into the room, and taking a seat at their small breakfast table.

"Well is a bit of an understatement." Hannah said, grinning from ear to ear.

"Yeah. We're amazing. Really. It's like a door's been swung wide open, hell kicked in, and everything's flooded back. So many memories of our," Sam gestured towards

Hannah, "time together have come back to us. To remember how we met. To remember anything before being thrust into the world the way we were. To be able to *speak* to each other again. It's a gift. Thank you."

"What about-"

Hannah took Kaia's hand before she could finish her question, "We take the bad with the good. That's life. And we are thankful for the good you have helped bring back into our lives." Her smile lit up the room, and warmed Kaia's heart.

"I'm so happy this worked out as well as it did for you guys. I was worried about you."

"And we know you still are. Go get some sleep, you look like you've been up, well, for forty-eight hours." Sam smiled at her.

Kaia checked her watch, and it was almost 9 pm.

"I should see to the troops before I-" Kaia stood up to leave, but almost fell right back down as a wave of dizziness washed over her. The women jumped up, ready to catch her, but she grabbed onto the back of the chair, managing to steady herself.

"You are ready to collapse. Let us handle it." Hannah said.

Kaia blinked her eyes to clear her vision before responding, "Get Lauren and Steven to help you."

"We will, now go."

Kaia nodded and left, thankful for their offer. Everything was becoming blurry, and she knew she would pass out the second her head hit the pillow.

Kaia stumbled several times walking to her room. She had been fighting so hard to stay awake, and now that she was ready to rest, it was as though all the exhaustion hit her at once.

"Woah there!"

A voice, the sound of feet shuffling, the thud of her body falling against the wall.

Kaia tried to speak, tried to lift her head up, but it was as if something was fighting her from the inside.

"I don't..."

She repeated the two words over and over, the rest of her thought slurring and trailing off.

"Hey. Kaia. It's me, Ben."

"Ben?... I..."

"You don't what?"

Hands catching her. Vision fading.

"I don't understand..."

Darkness taking over.

Falling further.

The jolt of becoming dead weight in the hands that held her.

And then...

Everything...

Went...

Black.

Chapter 12

It was dark, and Kaia had to blink her eyes several times before things began to focus. She could make out the silhouette of a bed above her own, and could hear someone gently snoring. Then, suddenly breaking the silence, screams came, echoing inside her skull, bouncing around like a rogue ball. Kaia groaned and held her hands to her head. Finally, the screams faded, and she banged a fist on the bed above her. No response. She thumped again, harder this time. Still no response.

Giving up on that endeavor Kaia sat up, and her head span. Swinging her legs over the edge of the bed and groaning, she rested her elbows on her thighs and pressed her hands to her temples, rubbing at them in an attempt to ease the pain in her aching head. Just as the pain began to settle the screams came back tenfold. It felt like they were trying to rip through her, and just as suddenly as they came they stopped again.

Kaia slowly stood up, careful of her spinning head, holding onto the bedpost. As she rose and looked around the room, confusion played across her face. She recognized where she was, but it didn't make sense. That desk, the metal door with the small window, the bunk bed! Kaia turned around, faster than her head agreed with, and was shocked by the sight before her. In the upper bunk, fast asleep was Lauren, and in the lower bunk, fidgeting and eyelids flickering, was herself. Only a decade younger.

"What the..."

Kaia grabbed the sides of her head and dropped to her knees, she didn't know how much longer she could take it. She sat there for several minutes, breathing slowly, trying to drive to screams out and comprehend what was happening.

Then it hit her. Slowly she tilted her head up until she was looking back at her sleeping body. She was back in the past somehow, and she knew exactly what night this was.

"Dean..." She whispered.

Kaia tried to call out to her husband, but got nothing outside of his agonized screams; at least they'd stopped rattling her brain nigh unto death. Kaia tiptoed over to the door and looked out the small window. One of

Grady's Authorities was standing at the end of the hall a few doors down keeping guard.

"Shit..."

Kaia looked around the room again, and her gaze swept over Lauren's sleeping body. She walked over to the bed and shook her, trying to wake her up, but she didn't respond. Kaia gave up. She wasn't really there, so there was no real reason for Lauren to wake up. But there was no doubt in her mind that if Lauren were awake she would see her. Kaia returned to the door, checking the window again; the Authority was still there.

"Well, here goes nothing."

Kaia gently pushed the door open and, staying crouched, closed the door as quietly as possible, then turned down the hallway opposite the Authority. Once around the corner Kaia stood up, looked behind her, and breathed a sigh of relief.

That was almost too easy.

As she turned back around she bumped into someone. It was a young Hannah, no older than fourteen.

"Please don't hurt me. I'm sorry I-"

"Wait, what? Hurt you? I..." Kaia trailed off, the fear in the girl's eyes struck a nerve that hadn't been struck in a long time. It was the same fear she'd seen in the other youth's eyes, in her own eyes, that drove her to escape.

"Just get back to your room, carefully. Don't let anyone see you."

Hannah stood there in shock, staring at the woman.

"Go." Kaia gave her a nudge, and she took off down the hall.

Kaia watched Hannah run into a room, and close the door quietly behind herself.

Another wave of pain crashed though Kaia's head and she shook it off; knowing what it was made it easier to ignore. Kaia stealthily maneuvered through the halls and rooms of the facility, avoiding everyone she came across.

It took some time to navigate the facility, going mostly off of instinct and the innate feeling of where Dean's screams were coming from, but eventually she came to a large set of steel doors at the end of a dimly lit concrete hallway. As she got closer she was able to truly hear Dean's screams of anguish. There was also a voice whose words were muffled by the thickness of the doors. But even though she couldn't make out what was being said, the words were distinctly carried by a thick Southern accent.

Kaia crept closer and closer to the door until her ear was pressed against it, and just as the voice became easier to hear everything stopped. There had been a buzzing sound that she hadn't noticed before, but now that it was gone everything was eerily silent. Then the Southern man spoke again, only this time there was no mistaking what he was saying.

"I own you boy. You and everyone else here. Don't forget that."

Heavy footsteps drew closer to the door, and before Kaia knew what was happening she was face to face with the man who had tortured her husband. The man who had done unspeakable things to her, her friends, and countless others. Grady Andrews.

Ben burst into Seong's office carrying Kaia's limp body.

"What happened!?" The doctor cried, as she rushed to his side.

Charles was close behind, quickly jumping in to help Ben with the dead weight of their General -for which he was grateful.

"I don't know. I just saw her stumbling down the hall. She passed out before I could get anything out of her."

They followed Seong back into the room where Dean was, and lifted Kaia up onto a bed beside him.

"Did she say anything? Anything at all?"

"She said, 'I don't understand.'"

Ben held his hands up helplessly with the useless information he had given, "That's it."

Seong nodded, and the two looked upon their Generals' unconscious bodies, helpless to do anything about it.

"What do we do now?" Ben stammered.

"We do what we can. You and your partner should take command, along with Miss. Darkholme and Miss. Adler-"

Ben interrupted, "Wouldn't Jack or Gerard be better for taking temporary command?"

"And who would replace them in the field? No. It's best they stay in charge of their squads."

"Looks like you just got promoted." Charles interjected.

Ben's mouth dropped, he didn't know what to say.

Seong continued, ignoring his evident shock, "Tell the soldiers what has happened. That our Generals are out of commission temporarily. I'll have someone watch them and we'll get back to work on decrypting the data Lauren and Steven brought us. Hopefully I'll find something helpful. In the meantime... you keep fighting the good fight."

Ben nodded, looked over at Dean and Kaia's bodies, then left to find Freddie, Sam, and Hannah.

"What are you doing down here?"

Kaia came up with something on the fly, hoping that it would assuage the situation she had found herself in.

"I was on patrol, my first time alone, and I got a little lost. Sir."

Grady, resting one hand on his belt buckle, spat out the splinters of a toothpick he had been chewing on the ground at Kaia's feet. He took a menacing step forward, pulled out a fresh toothpick, and popped it between his teeth. Their eyes stayed locked on one another for several seconds before he looked her up and down, and the gruff look on his face contorted into lust.

"Ya know miss," He said, rolling the toothpick between his tongue and teeth, "I'd be happy to escort you back. If you know what I mean." He took another step towards her, and she could feel his breath on her neck.

"As tempting as that sounds," Kaia stepped towards him, lightly running her fingers up and down his arm as she spoke, "I think I can find my way back. I just got a little distracted is all. Besides, I should probably stick to my duties. Wouldn't want to piss off the big man upstairs. If you know what I mean." Kaia smiled coyly and took a big step back to find the wall immediately behind her.

He chuckled a little and rubbed at the stubble on his chin as he spoke, "I like you. Come see me in my office when you're off duty." He started walking away, but turned back to look at Kaia after a few steps, "Oh, and I'm the big man upstairs." He winked and continued down the hall.

Kaia didn't move again until she saw him disappear around the corner, upon which a shudder of disgust and anger washed over her body. She slowly pushed the door open, peering around the corners to make sure no one else was around, then snuck in and closed the door quietly behind her.

It was a dark, musty room that reeked of charred flesh, and dim lights flickered across the room giving it a haunted house feel. Towards the back of the room a light bulb on a long wire swung back and forth, only revealing what was under it when it reached the apex of its arc.

Upon seeing what the light revealed she ran forward and slid to her knees, trembling. Before her, slumped over and held in place with restraints, sat her unconscious and severely burned husband. His younger body wasn't as muscular as he is now, but was still handsome in its youth. Just like she remembered.

Kaia ran her hands over his exposed arms and felt the bubbly lines where he had been electrocuted. Her vision began flashing in and out, flipping between the faint scars she'd felt on his arms in the present and now, to when they were put there.

Her hands reached the thick leather restraints held in place by large metal buckles -they were bright with the heat from the repeated electrocutions, and her eyes followed the wires that were embedded into the bubbling flesh on his body. She followed them all the way to a large machine against the back wall. The source of the torture.

She peeled the wires from his skin, cringing at the sticky sound his flesh made as they came free. She tossed the wires away, then went to work on the restraints.

Once he was free Kaia lifted his head up gently, and spoke softly to him, trying to rouse him from his pain-induced sleep. When he didn't rouse she turned to their ability.

Dean, you need to wake up. Find my voice. Follow it. Come home to me.

He still didn't show any sign he'd heard her.

Kaia took a deep breath and tried again.

Janna had just joined Seong and Charles in their effort to uncover the information within the intel from Lauren and Steven, when one of their colleagues, a plain looking woman, came bursting through the door. Seong looked up, desperate hope in her eyes.

"Are they awake?"

"No, but I think you should see this."

"Janna, come with me. Charles, stay here and keep at it."

Charles nodded, and Janna followed Seong back into the room where Mr. and Mrs. Whittaker lay.

"Alright, what is it?" Seong asked.

"Look." The woman pushed her glasses up on her nose, then pointed at them.

"I don't see anything." Seong sighed. Her tiredness was increasing her agitation, and she blew a stray strand of hair out of her eyes.

"Look closely."

And she did; they were twitching slightly.

"So?" Seong asked.

"They're movements are exactly the same." Janna's voice broke the tenseness in the air, "Maybe she's getting through to him somehow."

Seong pondered this for a moment, then dismissed the doctor who had fetched them.

"Alright, stay with them. Monitor them closely, keep track of everything. Get me when they wake up."

Seong left, and Janna pulled up a chair in front of the couple. Pulling out a notepad and pen she began taking detailed notes. Every change in heart rate, oxygen intake, body movement, and sound that took place over the next three hours was documented thoroughly.

Chapter 13

Freddie chased after Ben down the barracks hall while pulling a shirt on. Ben had burst into his room shortly after he had showered, saying 'come with me now', and just left.

"What is going on?" Freddie had caught up, and now stood in Ben's way. "Would ya just slow down, for one second."

"Look, just follow me, I'd rather just say this once. With everyone." Ben said, a strangely anxious look taking over his usually confident face.

Freddie sighed in defeat and ran a hand through his wet hair, pulling it out of his eyes, before following again. Ben spotted Sam and Hannah walking down the hall just ahead of them, laughing and chatting closely.

"Hannah! Sam! Wait up!"

The women turned around to see Ben jogging towards them.

"What's up?" Hannah asked, a big smile on her face.

"Something has happened, I need you and Sam to come with us."

The women's smiles lessened, "What's going on?" Sam asked.

Ben's eyes fell to the ground, and he just kept walking.

"Just come on." Freddie said as he walked past the girls, "He hasn't told me shit either."

Everyone available report to The Lobby immediately.

An announcement played over the speakers throughout the base, repeating the sentence three times.

Ben waited silently for everyone to arrive, and as the room quickly filled he stood outside the door for a moment to go over what he was going to say. He took a deep breath before stepping back in, and his eyes met Freddie's. He was clearly exasperated, and Ben tried to say sorry with the eye contact.

Everyone looked over to him as he entered, wondering what this could possibly be about. Ben cleared his throat and began his speech.

"Thank you everyone for coming on such short notice. There has been an incident involving the Generals. They are... for lack of better words, currently out of commission."

Lauren and Steven stepped out from the crowd, and into immediate view of Sam and Hannah.

What's going on? Lauren reached out to Hannah.

No clue.

"Dr. Lee and her team are taking great care to ensure they have a speedy recovery. In the meantime we all need to work together to ensure that this place stays standing in their absence. Myself, Freddie, Sam, and Hannah will act as stand-in-Generals in the meantime. We will run the B.O meetings, and see the departure and returns of the day and night crews. We will keep fighting, and we will make them proud. I am sorry I don't have more information as to what happened, but when I know, you'll know. Thank you for your time."

Lauren and Steven approached the four Captains as everyone filed out.

"We will help you in leading these people, and in ensuring their safety."

Ben looked at the woman who spoke, and recognized her from the other day. "I'm sorry, I don't believe we've had a proper introduction. What's your name?" Ben asked, holding out his hand to shake.

"My name is Lauren Greene, and this is my husband Steven Rhee."

"We can vouch for them. They're good people, good fighters. Old friends of Dean and Kaia, and new friends of ours." Hannah said, smiling at the couple.

"Well then welcome, I appreciate the help."

"Ben, we'll make sure we're back for the p.m-B.O meeting, but we have to do something. Just the four of us." Sam said, gesturing towards Hannah, Lauren, and Steven.

"I'll you see then." Ben looked mentally exhausted, and Hannah sympathized; he never was one for public speaking.

Chapter 14

Sam knocked on the door to Dr. Lee's office, and it was opened promptly. They were greeted by Seong gesturing for everyone to come in before returning to her desk -littered with coffee cups again.

"How are they doing?" Lauren asked.

"They're stable. That's about all the information I have. It's hard to diagnose something when you don't know what the cause is. Janna is keeping close watch over them, and as soon as anything changes we'll know."

"What about the two men Dean and Kaia brought to you? Are they well?" Sam asked. The concern in her eyes made it evident that she knew these two men, and it was only clear to her as to how now that the swipe had been undone. But it was a look no one else caught.

"Well actually, there's a bit of a story to them. Their names are Chris Mikami and Kurtis Gard. When Kaia checked in on them earlier she found that they were also chipped, like yourselves, and she ordered them to be removed. They are recovering as we speak."

They must have been the two others who had escaped before Dean and Kaia. Steven spoke to Lauren.

"Can we see them?" Sam asked.

"Of course." Seong emptied the cup closest to her, tucked some stray hairs behind her ears, then led them to the room where the men were resting.

As they entered the room something suddenly clicked in Steven's mind, and he was surprised he hadn't realized it earlier.

"I know these men."

Sam and Hannah looked between themselves and Steven, shocked and curious as to how, worried for a moment that they still had traces of the swipe.

"They were in a couple of the same classes as me for a while. Then one day they just disappeared. I just figured Grady had carted them off to some other part of the facility."

One of the men groaned and pushed himself up along the small cot, resting his head against the wall.

"Steven?"

"Kurtis!"

"Ungh... What's going on? It feels like I went twelve rounds with a steel wall and lost." Kurtis rubbed at his

his head, wincing with every movement from the bruises that covered his body.

Chris grumbled, and slowly pushed himself up, leaning on his arm.

"Steven? Man, is that you?"

"Yeah. Long time no see. You look like shit."

The two men chuckled, and Sam and Hannah stood off to the side, waiting for Steven's reunion to finish. Chris caught the women out of the corner of his eye and fell into a stunned silence.

"You..." He whispered, grunting as he pushed himself off the bed. "We thought you were dead."

"We were as good as dead." Sam's voice cracked, she couldn't hold the tears back anymore, and as they trickled down her cheeks Chris enveloped her in a big hug.

"What happened to you? We met with Claire one night, and she told us you'd just vanished." Kurtis said, walking up beside the three.

"We got swiped and sent out into the world to fend for ourselves." Hannah said.

"Swiped?" Chris asked, letting Sam go.

"All of our memories, just gone. Childhood, parents, friends, family. Everything Grady did to us. Just gone. All we had was each other while we were out there. Eventually made our way here. Just got everything back a couple days ago. How's Claire? Is she here somewhere too?"

The glimmer of hope in Sam's eyes brought her an immediate pang of guilt as she saw the pain and regret in the men before her. It was more than that though: sorrow, anger, hatred, fear.

"She's still with him. For the first couple days after we got out we were still able to maintain contact with her. But it's been six years since we've heard anything from her, and I'm beginning to lose hope. The only thing keeping the hope alive is that I can sense I'm getting through to her, but she's just not responding. It's difficult to explain."

Chris' eyes had welled up with tears, and his voice cracked by the time he was done speaking. His sister was his whole world, and it was all he could do not to tell himself it was his fault if she was dead.

Sam pulled Chris back into the hug and whispered in his ear, "If she is dead, it's not your fault. It's his."

Chapter 15

Kaia knelt on the ground at her husband's feet, her hands gripped tightly in the material of his pants. The whole situation was threatening to overwhelm her, so she took some deep breaths, and calmed herself until her knuckles were no longer white. Flexing her fingers, and her mind, Kaia focused like she never had before. She ignored her instinctive ability to use her telepathy with Dean, and dug deep into her brain; like when she tried to speak to Lauren over a decade ago. She latched onto that spot where the emotional met the primal part of the brain and bellowed into Dean's mind.

Dean! Wake up! Please! You have to wake up!

She felt his leg quiver underneath her hands, the first sign of life he'd given her since she'd found him like this, and it gave her renewed hope.

Dean, please! I need you to come back to me. Please.

She begged into his mind.

Dean...

Soon that leg quiver turned into an arm twitch, then a hand spasm, and an eyelid flutter, then a low grumble -a dry, raspy sound that came from deep within his throat. Kaia looked up with glossed over eyes, one hand squeezing his, the other running through his hair.

Dean blinked his eyes and looked around, wincing when his burnt skin crinkled. "Kaia? ... What's happening?"

Mrs. Whittaker took a deep breath before responding, "Now, this is gonna sound kinda crazy. Or a lot crazy... We're inside your head. Trapped in some kind of memory coma. You never woke up after the chips were removed. Two days later I got pulled into it as well."

"How?"

"I don't know. The last thing I remember is talking to Sam and Hannah, then I woke up here." Kaia stood up, offering a hand to help Dean up. "We need to get out of here. We need to figure out how to wake up and get back home."

Dean reached out for her hand, gritting his teeth as his burned skin rubbed against itself, and as he pushed himself out of the chair the image of his youthful, albeit burned, body faded away, becoming the sculpted wall of muscle he had grown into. Dean was the man again, and with the chip removed he felt a flood of power come rushing back. And as it did he realized something that the other's had yet to sit down long enough to figure out. The chips didn't give them their ability, they controlled it, and there was so much more to it than just being able to communicate within themselves.

The feeling started at the base of his skull, like a spark forcing itself to ignite. Small jolts of pressure fired from that base into the rest of his body until he could feel it in his fingertips and toes. He felt as though his whole body was truly alive for the first time. Everything was clearer, and his thoughts came with logic and speed, sorting through any and all possible outcomes of the situation he was in. Even the stale air of the musty room they were in felt more alive against his skin. All of his senses were heightened, and the possibilities that had been opened up to him were bursting through his mind.

He lifted his head calmly, with a sense of purpose, and he could see tiny specks of dust fluttering down from the ceiling. Dean tilted his head to the side and held his hand out, catching some of the falling particles.

"What is it?" Kaia asked.

"Footsteps, and lots of them."

"How did you-"

"Listen."

"I am listening." She said, a slight irritation in her voice.

"No," Dean went behind her, placing his hands on her shoulders. He brought his mouth to her ear and whispered, "Really listen."

Kaia took a deep breath, closed her eyes, and did as he said. It started as a light vibration, slowly getting stronger and stronger until everything became clearer in every sense of the word. The feeling of his hands on her shoulders, though the material of her henley was between them, she could feel him like she never had before. Small sparks began bursting through her body, enlightening her world and everything in it. She opened her eyes, and let it all in. The dust floating down from above was the first thing she noticed; she could feel a small tickle as the particles brushed against her skin. Then the vibration bounced through her body like electricity, awakening the abilities that had been forcibly activated within her mind, only to be immediately blocked. Kaia's mind was truly alive, and her connection with Dean became stronger. No longer was it just an ease of communication, his every thought, idea, emotion, and facial expression -right now it was a gentle smile- could be sensed by her mind, and vice versa. She could feel the sound of his heartbeat, and the expansion of his lungs with each breath he took. And she could hear the footsteps racing towards them.

She smiled, and he -still standing behind her- could see it clear as day in his mind's eye. Dean spun her around and kissed her, the passion so intense it seared through their bodies, creating a sensation of pure euphoria. Then the doors slammed open, and they turned to see fifty fully armed men and women with their guns pointed at them. Kaia hadn't gone as unnoticed as she thought.

Mr. and Mrs. Whittaker looked at them, smiling, as the crowd parted in the middle. The clicking of boot heels could be heard easily, but Dean and Kaia could hear so much more. The wet sound of something being chewed, gruff breathing, a snort, fingernails scratching a beard. Then he came in to view, Grady Andrews himself, his Southern accent as thick as they remembered.

"Tsk, tsk, tsk." He tutted as he walked towards the couple, but it was as if he only had eyes for Kaia. "You know girl, we could have had something special." The toothpick rolled across his lips, "Where's the boy?"

"He's right here." She said, her voice calm and serene as she directed an open palm towards Dean as though she were delivering a presentation.

Grady looked back and forth between her and the man she was claiming to be Dean.

"Maybe this will be more recognizable." Dean closed his eyes and conjured the image of his younger self onto his body.

He could feel the alarm coursing through Grady's body, and as he opened his eyes the conjuring crashed to the ground, shattering into a million pieces. Grady was rendered speechless, the toothpick fell from his gaping mouth, and he stumbled backward.

"Open fire." He said shakily, retreating into the crowd of his Authorities.

Kaia raised a hand, and drawing on the stale air of the room she manipulated it. Hardened it into a barrier between them and the barrage of bullets. Every one of them hit the invisible wall and dropped to the ground. With all the noise no one noticed that their bullets were being rendered useless.

Are you ready? Dean whispered in Kaia's mind.

Always. She smiled up at him.

Dean knew what he had to do. He could feel what was wrong within the depths of his mind, and knew that once he fixed that, Kaia would be safe too. He reached deep into his psyche and began rebuilding the cerebral bridge that connected his subconscious mind back to his unconscious body; that's what had been broken during the procedure and dragged him here.

I can't hold them back for much longer, Dean. What are you doing?

I almost have it.

"Cease fire!"

Grady had reappeared at the front of the line, and locked eyes with Kaia. She could see the fear and confusion evident in his face.

Got it.

The link was made, and suddenly they were back.

Janna had been writing frantically on her notepad. The monitors had been giving the strangest readings, and she didn't want to miss anything. Suddenly Dean and Kaia sat straight up in their beds, startling Janna. She jumped backward, dropping her pad and pen, and bringing a hand up to her mouth to stifle a gasp.

"Sorry." Kaia said, a slight chuckle in her throat.

Grady bolted upright in his bed, wide awake. He rushed to the room where Dean was being held. Throwing the doors open he saw the battered, broken boy sitting in the chair, his head hung down in unconsciousness. Grady, still confused, angered, and scared by what could only be explained as a dream, went over to the control panel and shocked Dean awake. The boy arched his back and screamed, and back in the bunk Kaia let out a scream that echoed it, causing Lauren to wake up.

Chapter 16

Chris and Kurtis sat with the others in Seong's office, getting caught up to speed on what was going on, and the procedure they had just gone through. They were just about to tell the group the story of how they'd escaped when the door came flying open, Janna on the other side of it looking like a deer in headlights. Everyone's heads turned, and Seong asked the question that was on everyone's mind.

"What is it? Is everything alright?"

"They're awake." The statement was simple, and there was a peaceful smile on her face. She left before there were any other questions or comments, and they all followed.

Kaia and Dean sat together on one of the beds, a sense of serenity emanating from them. Dean had propped himself up against the headboard, one leg hanging over the edge with his foot on the ground. Kaia sat likewise but leaning into Dean's chest, and their hands danced with each other, dust particles floating between their fingers.

Everyone came into the room at once, concern and curiosity shining from all of their faces.

We're fine. Kaia spoke peacefully into the minds of their friends.

"Dr. Grey," Kaia turned her gaze to Janna, "Thank you for watching over us." Her voice carried a level of calm that that seemed to affect everyone in the room, it was almost hypnotic.

Kaia stood up, and the particles that were dancing around the couple's hands dropped to the floor. Sam caught the movement out of the corner of her eye, and as she looked back up her eyes met Kaia's.

What happened to you two?

Kaia just smiled in response; explanations could wait.

Kaia stepped towards a man with an extremely thick muscular build, buzz cut sandy brown hair and a scruffy five o'clock shadow that hid the gentleness that shone from his dark brown eyes.

"Chris. I am glad to see you are in better condition than the last time I saw you."

"And I am glad to have that thing out of my head. We both are." He gestured to the man beside him.

He was a tall, lean man with a subtle muscular structure, short almost black hair that stood up in messy spikes easily, and hazel eyes that glinted dark orange when the light hit them.

"Thank you." Kurtis stepped forward and shook Kaia's hand.

"You're welcome."

Kurtis continued, "I have to ask though, how did you know we had them? We never told anyone where we came from. Almost told you guys when you introduced yourselves as escapees from Grady's facility when you first showed up, but decided against it."

"I noticed the scars behind your ears, the same ones we have."

Seong, silent up until now, spoke up, "I am glad to see you are well."

"Thank you. We had good people watching over us." Kaia smiled at her.

"Have you found anything useful in that intel yet?" Dean asked, joining Kaia's side.

"We actually do have a fair bit of news on that front." Seong perked up, and headed for the door, "If you'll follow me we have much to talk about."

The group followed Seong back to her office, and she led them into an antechamber. The small room was dimly lit, and resembled a miniature lecture hall, adorned with only desks, chairs, a projector, and a large whiteboard covering the back wall. There was a projected image on it, and it read, 'Project Deus'.

Everyone grabbed one of the chairs that were scattered around the room, and sat facing the board. Seong stood by the projector in the middle of the room, waiting for the sound of chair legs scraping the floor to stop before speaking.

"Project Deus, as everyone knows was developed by a young man named Grady Andrews."

The image on the projector flipped to a young adult. His jawline, nose, and eyes made him recognizable as Grady, but only just. He wore the demeanor of a boy genius bursting with hope at his 'breakthrough idea', but that boy was long gone. An insatiable desire to see his theories become a reality had changed him in every way. Beside his picture was a snippet from his original proposal, and it read:

> **"I believe that within the Endocrine System lies the potential for powerful capabilities that we've only dreamed of having. Starting with Jean Pierre Flourens, then William James and Boris Sidis, and finally Karl Lashley, the idea that**

we only use about 10% of our brain's ability has been a notion that has been firmly believed, and then firmly disproven. It is my belief that those men weren't as wrong as they were proven to be. I have spent all of my educational years dedicating myself to making sure that I am going after the correct potential to prove this theory true. I will be specifically looking at the Hypothalamus, and the Pituitary Gland of the Endocrine System, and given the right circumstances I know I can help mankind make its greatest leap forward in evolution since the Homo-Sapien. By tapping into that other 90% we could be so much more."

"We don't know much about him outside of this project, other than his extensive education in the scientific field. That and a strange sense of humor, given the name he chose for his Project."

"What do you mean?" Asked Chris.

"Deus is Latin for God." Kaia said quietly.

Seong nodded and continued speaking, "As we can see from his proposal, he strongly believed that with a few tweaks he could set evolution on a new 'Great Leap Forward'."

"Only it wasn't just a few tweaks." Dean whispered.

"He was a charismatic man, and considering his education, he was granted the necessary funding to run his Project easily. Unfortunately, he was as charismatic as he was insane. When scientists predicted the inevitable flare strike, Grady took the distraction as an opportunity to further his experimentations in unethical secrecy. Then when the flares did come it only got worse. We found files depicting the failures he experienced when he first turned to human trials."

The series of images Seong flipped through were nightmarish to say the least. Images of men and women, mostly adults but there were several young children, all dead. All with thick blood running from their eyes, ears, nose, and mouth.

"Autopsies showed that their brains had literally melted as a result of initial trials."

She flipped the projector once more to display a blank screen. Not wanting to leave the horrific images on display while she moved on was something everyone was thankful for.

"These experiments began in 2084, and it wasn't until 2088 that he had his first success. Four years of horrific deaths, and torture, just to lead to more unspeakable torture. We weren't able to find any information on that first success, but everything after that was based on him using fifteen to seventeen-year-olds in his experiments, and the results were finally successful. Progress was being made. Grady had found his tweak."

Seong flipped the projector to a new screen. It was a list that read:

Group A: Telepaths
Group B: Elementals
Group C: Cerebral Connectors
Group D: Kinetics
Group E: Telekinetics
Group F: Heightened sensors
Group G: Conjurers
Group H: Rapid reactors

"He began compiling a list of all the abilities that were surfacing, and decided that each ability should be isolated within certain subjects to be tested on in a controlled environment, and that's where the chips come into play. The chips that were inside you were designed to detect and isolate the telepathic ability that surfaced. Group A."

Seong paused a moment before continuing, "Groups B through H, the other abilities that you will all now begin experiencing are: elemental manipulation, cerebral bridge building, kinetic energy buildup, telekinesis, heightened senses, conjuring, and rapid reaction time."

"Dean and I experienced most of these during his coma, but I can already feel them fading." Kaia said.

"In times of stress the mind and body resort to instinct, and within you," Seong was referring to all of them, "that instinct is powerful."

"The cerebral connecting. That must have been what was fighting to take over inside me when I blacked out. I woke up inside his coma. How did you get us out?"

"I was trapped in that coma because something in my head had broken. My subconscious had detached itself while I was out. I had to rebuild the... cerebral connection," Dean looked up at the board as he said those two words, "that linked my subconscious mind back to my unconscious body. And when I did that, you were released from the same instinct. Man, did I sound as crazy as I think I just did?"

"Yes." Steven said, laughing with him.

Seong cleared her throat and continued speaking, "I believe that given time your minds will reawaken to the evolution that has happened within you. I think the best way for it to happen is to embrace it as it comes, don't fight it."

"What about the creatures? Is there anything about them in the files? Did he build them?" Dean asked.

"Yes, I was actually just coming up to that." Seong switched the image on the projector again, "He calls them 'Grady's Hunters'."

The picture was a prototype drawing of the creatures with their name scrawled beside it.

"He designed them to detect the chips within a certain range and target them."

"So the more chips in close vicinity of one another, the stronger the signal." Kaia said.

"Exactly."

"Well, that kills two birds with one stone. At least we can fight together again." Dean said.

That comment earned him several puzzled glances from around the room.

"Kaia and I, we found that when we were out there fighting together, the creatur-Hunters, came at us with more ferocity than when we were alone. With the chips gone, they can't detect us anymore."

"They can't hunt us anymore." Kaia said, pointing out the obvious reason for their name.

"And to kill them?" Dean asked, wishful thinking driving his hope that the answer would be as simple as the other one.

"They were built to be indestructible. But I was able to find was a code that once input into their operating systems would shut them down. I was going to test it out on the one you brought in tomorrow."

There was a moment of silence, then Kaia spoke in that way she did when she talked to herself. "The emp triangulation plan. I know it'll be harder now that we've lost our bait, but it's still the best chance we have for being able to incapacitate them. At least we can make it permanent with this code." Kaia's train of thought stopped, and she looked up at Seong, the tone of her voice going back to normal, "Have you heard any updates from Gi?"

"Not yet."

"What are you talking about?" Lauren asked.

Kaia turned in her chair to face Lauren, "Before you and Steven showed up, Dean had captured one of the Hunters; tranquilized it and cut its limbs off. We were able to dissect it, and we came up with a plan. To lure them all, or at least most of them, into one area, and use an emp triangulation to shut them down long enough to kill them." Kaia said.

"And by bait you mean...?" Lauren asked.

"Us." Kaia said, referring to herself and Dean, "But with the chips removed..."

"I actually have an idea for that." Seong said.

Everyone's gaze shifted from Kaia and Dean, back to Seong.

"I can implant all of the chips I removed from you, into the carcass that Dean brought in. If you can get it out into the field, the Hunters should all flock to it."

Everyone sat in silence as they contemplated the potential outcomes.

"How soon can we do this?" Kaia asked.

"Whenever the techs have the emp equipment ready. There is a catch though."

"Of course there is." Kaia said, her jovial tone taking away the exasperated condescension of the words.

"I won't be able to activate the chips once it's out there. I'll have to activate them in here."

"So we'll basically be carrying a ticking time bomb with no way of knowing when it will go off." Dean said.

"Technically, well, yes." Seong said.

"Great." There was sarcasm in his voice, but his demeanor quickly softened as his gaze landed on Kaia, and he saw her smile.

"Well, what do you say? Til death do us part?" He laughed.

"You know it." Kaia winked at him exaggeratedly.

"I'll speak with Gi soon, but since I haven't heard from him yet I can only assume it will still be some time before the equipment is ready. In the meantime I think you should work on harnessing and controlling your abilities." Seong said, shutting down the projector.

Kaia checked her watch, it read 8:48 pm.

We should go, the night crew will be waiting for us soon. She spoke to Dean, and he nodded in agreement.

Kaia stood up and faced everyone, "Seong makes a good point, that is definitely something we should make a priority. Dean and I will work out a plan for that tonight, then tomorrow hang back after the a.m-B.O meeting, and we'll go from there. Until then, enjoy your night off."

Everyone left without question, all eager to sit down, eat, shower and sleep.

Go, I'll meet you there. Kaia kissed Dean on the cheek, and he left.

It was just her and Seong left in the room.

"Did you manage to find any information on the facility? Specifically blueprints of, and maps leading to, it? If I'm going to lead an attack against him, which I will, I'll need that." Kaia said.

"Not yet, but there's still plenty of documents to go through. If it's there I'll find it."

"I know you will." Kaia said.

Chapter 17

By the time Dean arrived at The Lobby Ben and Freddie were already sending the day crew to the equipment room, and getting report from the Colonels who had been out that day. Jack, your stereotypical handsome military man with the chiseled jaw, short brown hair and hazel eyes, was particularly close to Amara. He was unconsciously smiling and looking at her whenever she spoke. Amara, who was pretending not to notice the looks, was a beautiful lithe woman with ivory pale skin, striking long red hair that was always worn down with one small tight braid that hung by her right ear, and dark eyes. Then there was Sasha, a mocha colored beauty with dark blue eyes, and enough power behind her toned muscle to kick Jack's ass; he'd seen it happen once or twice in training.

Dean leaned against the door frame as he watched them, and decided now was as good a time as any to test out some of his new found abilities. He conjured the image of a regular soldier onto himself and stepped into the room. Moments later the Night Colonels entered the room.

“Man, you always get to go out with the ladies. Next time you get Ki.”

“Hey.”

“Nothing against you man, it’s just. Well, you ain’t no Sasha.”

Dean smiled at the banter that passed between Ki, and Gerard. Ki was an average looking man with distinct Korean features who always kept the left side of his head shaved, but what he lacked in physical stature he made up for in speed. Dean had once seen him roll and dodge his way between the limbs of three different Hunters to the point that they had tangled amongst themselves so bad they wound up impaling each other. Gerard was another handsome man like Jack, with the same hair, but with bright green eyes. He wasn’t quite as built as Jack, but he made up for it in height, standing at almost seven feet. Gerard walked up to Sasha and wrapped an arm around her waist, to which she responded with a playful elbow to the side.

“Did you see that? She can’t resist me.” Gerard leaned over to Ki and whispered, humor coating his voice.

Gerard and Sasha shared a smile, one that shone from the eyes as well.

"Try not to scuff her up this time." Sasha said, handing her MP5 over to Gerard.

She walked away before he could respond, waving behind her as she left the room, and Gerard stared after her. He shook his head, looking away when the view was obstructed by Jack's arse walking away, Amara close by.

"Any word on Generals' Whittaker yet?" Ki asked Ben.

"Not yet no. Hopefully I'll have better news in the- Kaia!"

Ben's face lit up at the sight of her walking through the door. Dean pulled himself to the back of the room, and let the conjuring fade.

"You're a sight for sore eyes."

Ben forgot all formalities and pulled her in for a hug. Kaia smiled and returned the gesture, thankful that he had been there when she fell victim to her own abilities.

"How's Dean?" Ben asked.

"He should have been here already, he left before I did."

"I'm right here." Dean spoke up, stepping out of the shadows.

"Holy shit. How long have you been there for?" Ben had a comical look of confusion on his face.

"Since Jack, Amara, and Sasha were still here. You were doing so well, I didn't want to interrupt."

Dean flashed a mischievous smile and joined Kaia's side, putting an arm around her waist, his hand resting on her hip.

"Well I've had my fill of leading meetings, you can have your job back." Ben said.

"Why don't you and Freddie head to dinner. We'll take it from here." Kaia smiled at him.

"You got it boss."

Generals' Whittaker finished up the p.m-B.O meeting, went for dinner, then headed back to their room.

Chapter 18

Kaia pulled her hair out of its pony tail, and scratched her scalp, shaking her hair out at the same time. She walked out of closet, sporting a tank top and boy-cuts, and closed her eyes as she flopped down on the bed. She lay there for a moment, just enjoying the peace that came with the comfort of her bed. From the bathroom she could hear Dean turn the shower on and get in.

Kaia rolled over on the bed, got up, then snuck into the bathroom. The steam was just beginning to fog up the mirror when lifted herself up to sit on the edge of the sink's counter. Dean started to hum, the sound was low and deep. Kaia recognized what it was he was humming, and smiled as she began to sing along.

"Wise men say, only fools rush in.
But I can't help falling in love with you.
Oh shall I stay?
Would it be a sin,

If I can't help falling in love with you."

Her voice gained slightly more volume as she went and Dean could hear her now. He smiled, continuing to hum as though he hadn't noticed her yet; he didn't want her to stop.

"Oh like a river flows surely to the sea

Darling so it goes some things are meant to be.

Oh take my hand, take my whole life too

For I can't help falling in love with you."

Dean pulled the shower curtain open a little bit as quietly as possible. He saw Kaia sitting there gently swaying back and forth, singing along to his humming. He leaned his head against the wall of the shower gazing at her, his eyes shining with pure adoration.

Kaia glanced over, saw him watching her, and reached her hand out gesturing him to come over to her. As he stepped over she pulled him closer with her legs, wrapping them around him. Her arms encircled his shoulders, and their mouths met. Dean ran his hands down the length of her back, his fingers closing around the hem of Kaia's tank top, and lifted it up over her head. She hopped down off the counter and kicked off her boy-cuts. Her fingers danced across Dean's chest to his shoulder, and down his arm to his hand. She led him back into the shower, and the water cascaded around them as they continued their intimacy.

The sounds of their arousal and passion echoed off the bathroom walls, and the fog on the mirror grew ten-fold. By the time it was over the exhaustion that they had felt before was replaced with satisfied sleepiness.

Dean used one hand to lean against the wall, the other to run through Kaia's hair. They stood close to each other, and the movements of their chests expanding with each breath caused their skin to brush against one another. Kaia looked up and kissed Dean gently, savoring the moment as their lips lingered on each other.

You, are, amazing.

Ditto. Kaia winked exaggeratedly at her husband before stepping out, wrapping a towel around herself, and heading back to bed.

Dean shut off the water, staring at her legs as she walked away. He quickly dried himself off, then pulled on a pair of loose pajama pants. Dean went to the mirror and wiped some of the fog off so he could see his reflection. He began looking over the scars on his biceps, something he hadn't done in a long time. His fingers traced over them gently, and flashes of what happened that night seared through his mind. Dean closed his eyes, took a deep breath, and left the bathroom, flipping the light off as he went.

"Thanks for warming up the bed." Dean said, wrapping his arms around Kaia.

"You're so cold!"

Kaia squirmed in his arms, and they laughed. She eventually found herself lying face to face with her husband, and the laughter died down, but the smiles stayed.

Do you have any thoughts on how to get these abilities of ours to kickstart? Kaia asked as she nestled into Dean's body.

I was thinking the old simulation room.

Oh my god, that's brilliant! I'd almost forgotten about that place.

Same here, It's been a while since we've been down there.

Chapter 19

After everyone had come and gone from the a.m-B.O meeting Dean and Kaia led the group to the far end of the base.

"So what's the plan?" Lauren asked.

"It's better if you just see it." Kaia said.

They walked down long stretches of hallway: past the barracks, and the gymnasium, past the dining hall, and The Lab, and finally past an elevator that led to the sub-basement level. Everyone, excluding Lauren and Steven as they hadn't been there, had figured out where they were headed to by that point. After all, there was only one place left to get to.

At the end of the hall was a simple metal door with a round light at the top. It shone green indicating that the room was safe to enter. As they went through the door Lauren and Steven stared in awe at the sheer size of the room. If the door was simple, the room was anything but. It was magnificent in size, and from inside the door looked like it was built for dwarves. The floor was a flat disc surrounded by seamless metal walls that stretched up into a dome-shaped ceiling.

Kaia and Dean stopped in the middle of the room, turning to face them.

"I hope you're all well rested. For those of you who haven't been in here before," Kaia gestured to Lauren and Steven, "this is the simulation room. It's where every newbie gets trained."

Kaia pulled out a remote control and pointed it towards the center of the ceiling. She began walking around them, speaking as she cycled through the different options the control gave her.

"In this room is every landscape, every circumstance, every enemy, and every situation you can think of. It adapts to you, draws on your memories and twists them, and you will have to outsmart it."

As each preview flashed by Lauren and Steven span trying to take everything in.

"No matter what happens in here you will be safe. Safe enough anyways. I can't say we've never had an injury in here before because we have, but be assured you will not die during a simulation. There is a fail safe that will kick in if your life is in real danger. This is how we will learn to use what we didn't want to begin with to destroy the man who did this to us."

Kaia took a deep breath before continuing, "Your success in the simulation will rely on your instinct and how you react with it." She clicked the remote one last time and suddenly they were standing in a glade surrounded by eight strange glowing orbs of emerald light, and trees that were almost as wide as they were tall.

"Our instincts are the most important thing that we have, because you won't always have a partner watching your back."

The glade filled with a bright emerald light that flared around each person, causing them to raise an arm to shield their eyes. When the light died, and they opened their eyes, they found themselves alone.

Learn to trust your instinct. Let the fear fall away, and take control.

Kaia's voice left them, and the feeling of complete and utter aloneness took over.

Sam looked down at the small gun in her hand, the one her father had given her when she was seven years old. Her mother had been attacked and killed one night on her way home from work, something her father had always fretted about, but she insisted she was fine. And she was fine, for a long time, until she wasn't. From that moment he was determined that his little girl would know how to protect herself. But what started as a way to ensure her ability to protect herself, quickly became a father-daughter bond, and they went on hunting trips together often. She was comfortable with the current model she had been given, a Beretta 687, and she peered down the barrel into the treeline ahead with determination. Suddenly everything flickered and the world went dark.

Sam lowered her gun subconsciously, and the sounds of growls and heavy breathing could be heard all around. Yellow eyes of all shapes and sizes began to glimmer in the darkness, and as she peered into one of the sets of eyes a dark cloud shaped into the likeness of a wolf that came bounding out of the tree line. The piercing yellow eyes locked onto Sam's throat as it came towards her. In the last second Sam brought her Beretta up and blasted the wild animal. The eyes popped, spraying blood into her face, and the shadow disappeared.

More shadow creatures emerged from the tree line -which had inexplicably encircled her. Shapes of wolves, bears, large wild turkeys, and boars came into view; all with the same crazed yellow eyes. One of the shadow bears was three feet away from her when she blasted its face with the small shotgun, and as its eyes exploded they all charged her. It was a maelstrom of shadows and exploding yellow lights that ended with arcs of blood spraying through the air.

She was messy at first: barely missing being rammed by the tusk of a boar, dodging just in the nick of time as the bear's jaws would have come clamping down on her head, sending a right hook out at the last possible moment as a flurry of oversized wings came towards her face. But soon it became easy, the reactions rapid and instinctual. Her breathing slowed down, and the sweat stopped dripping.

Bang. Bang.

Two wolves down.

A hard kick directed behind her.

A wild turkey knocked out of the air, and landing on a boar's tusk.

Bang. Bang.

A bear down, bringing with it a bird, and landing on another.

Bang. Bang.

Two boars down.

Bang.

A wolf.

A running jump off a boar's head, and grabbing a turkey out of the air to ram down onto its tusk.

Bang.

There goes the boar with it.

It went on like this for what seemed like forever, then as suddenly as it began it was over. Sam stood, staring into the darkness, and dropped the shotgun to the ground. The air around her was starting to ebb, and with it a bright emerald light was replacing the darkness. The light began to pulse until the brightness was too much to bear, and Sam had to bring her arms up to cover her eyes. As the final pulse of light went out a vibration shook through the ground. Sam slowly lowered her arms, and saw that she was back in the glade with the eight glowing orbs surrounding her. One was slightly dimmer than the rest.

Sam sat down cross-legged on the forest floor, and began exploring her own mind, digging for the other abilities that she knew lay buried in there. Suddenly Kurtis appeared by one of the emerald orbs, and it dimmed slightly.

"Welcome back." Sam smiled at him.

All that separated Kurtis from Claire was a wall. They would spend hours after lights out speaking with each other, sharing stories of what had happened that day. He wanted to escape, to take her away from this awful place, and go into hiding somewhere. They couldn't leave without Chris though, and neither of them had seen him in almost a month. Claire's hope was fading, all she could think about was Chris, and the less she paid attention in her classes the worse it was for her.

Kurtis had a fire burning inside him that just kept igniting every time she told him what they'd done to her. All he wanted in this very moment was to break down the wall and hold her tight, tell her that everything would be okay, that they'd find Chris, and get out.

And that's exactly what he was going to do.

Kurtis' skin began to vibrate, and his hands fluttered against the cold floor. It didn't take long for the vibrations in his body to spread to the walls and floor around him. Kurtis was building up a level of kinetic energy within the room that the materials had never experienced before. Even an earthquake wouldn't have moved them, but this was different.

Cracks spread throughout the concrete like a river breaking free, and Kurtis thought his body would burst at any moment. He steadied his breathing and allowed the power to take over his body. A blast echoed out from the flutter of his hands, bringing the wall between himself and Claire crumbling down. He stood up and stepped over the rubble, pulled Claire into his arms, wrapping them around her like he'd never let go.

All too quickly a group of Authorities came bursting into the destroyed room. Kurtis looked up, grinning, as his skin began to vibrate once more. He moved Claire to safety behind him and counted.

One, two, three, four... ten. Easy.

One of them stepped forward, and Kurtis let his power free. Speeding from one to the next he took them out with a speed and velocity that saw them all drop to the ground at once. The last thing Kurtis saw before a bright emerald light consumed his world was Claire's smile.

It took longer than he'd care to admit to realize he was now looking at Sam's smiling face. The simulation was over, and he missed Claire more than ever in that moment.

A high-pitched beeping woke Lauren out of a deep sleep, and her eyes burned when she opened them. The room was filling up with smoke, the same room she'd spent years as a child hiding from nightmares in. She rubbed her eyes with the base of her palms, and remembered what she had come home to the night of the fire. This was the reason she had wound up in the orphanage, this was how they died, and now she had to survive it. She opened them back up, squinting at first, and saw that the smoke was coming from under the closed door. She walked over to it, arms hovering in front of her face in an attempt to keep the smoke away from her eyes and mouth. She pressed her hand up against the door and it leapt right back off. Lauren shook her hand, trying in vain to cool it off, but the intense heat had already burned the skin from her palm. Pulling the sheet from the bed she ripped a strip free and wrapped it around her hand. While tying up the makeshift bandage she walked over to the window and looked out; there was rain beating down on it.

Too high to jump. I'll die on impact.

Can't climb the roof, it's too steep... and wet.

Lauren looked around to see if there was anything that could help her.

I could wrap the blanket around myself for protection...

It's too thin it'll go up in flames, and take me with it...

The smoke had thickened dramatically, blocking her vision. Lauren covered her face, coughing into her arm as she reached for the window. She opened it just as the wind picked up, and the smoke raced for the open air as rain sprayed into the room.

Flames started to flick in and out from underneath the door.

It's now or never girl, think of something.

Lauren looked around for something large enough to catch the water in. She rummaged through the closet until she found a small laundry basket. Lauren held it out the window, closing her eyes as the power of the rain beat down on her face. She turned around to see what she had caught.

Nothing.

The rain and wind were too chaotic to catch more than a few useless drops. She chucked the basket at the wall and sat down under the window at a loss.

Think... Think...

What if there was a way to direct the rain at the fire?

Lauren stood up and faced the open window. She concentrated until she could see each individual droplet of rain.

Control the flow of air... control where the rain goes.

Lauren backed away from the window, fixating all of her energy on the chaos that surrounded her, willing it to tame to her needs.

Slowly a tunnel of water started to form from the window to the door. The wood of the door was beginning to pop and split under the pressure of the heat, and the bright orange of the flames could be seen easily through the small cracks. Soon there was a torrent of water flowing from the window to the door. Lauren grabbed the rest of the sheet and wrapped it around her uninjured hand. She twisted the door handle, and it burst open, crashing into her.

Lauren flew backward from the impact, crumpling into a pile against the far wall, and in the process lost all control of the elements. The water dropped to the floor, soaking the carpet, and the fire roared even higher. Lauren grunted as she forced herself to stand back up, using one arm to shelter her eyes from the maelstrom that was the room she was trapped in, and the other to hold herself up against the wall. The fire continued to grow, reaching for the ceiling, the window slammed open and shut with the wild ferocity of the wind, and rain sprayed in all directions.

Lauren threw all of her focus into the energy of the water, and as she raised her arms up, the rain that had soaked into the carpet came rising up like a wall. With one final effort she pushed the water forward, drowning out the inferno. With her energy spent she collapsed to the ground, hoping it was over.

Out of the corner of her eye she could see the door begin to glow again.

Oh come on.

As she lifted her head up she realized this was something else, something brighter and...

Green?

Emerald light pulsated throughout the room slamming the window and door open and shut, over and over.

Lauren covered her ears, and closed her eyes, burying her head in her knees, until suddenly it all fell silent. She slowly opened her eyes, and found herself sitting back in the glade with the balls of emerald light hanging in the air around her.

Steven had grown accustomed to the tight quarters of the ductwork in the facility, moving throughout it quietly and effortlessly. But something was wrong, it was quieter than usual, too quiet. Suddenly a bullet ripped through the section of ductwork beside him, barely missing him. Steven flinched with terror as he felt the air pressure caused by the bullet rush past his arm. Another bullet ripped through behind him, and another right in front of his face. Then a realization hit him.

I'm deaf?

Steven felt a vibration in the metal beneath him, and he looked back to see a man in full tactical gear, crawling towards him. He immediately sprung into action, speeding his way through the system of ductwork.

A bullet went through his left hand, and he cried out in pain, but not being able to hear the sound of his own voice renewed his fortitude. He chanced a glance back before pushing onwards; he had made good time. Steven pulled himself forward, slowing down only slightly to alleviate the pressure in his wounded hand. Steven's other senses were quickly gaining in strength, and upon noticing a grate out of the corner of his eye quickly changed his course of direction. Without missing a beat he swung around and kicked it out, then dropped to the room below. It was a drab room with only three points of entry: a door, a window, and the grate he had just come through.

He scanned the room for any kind of weapon, but the room was bare save for a ratchet old hospital bed with restraints fixed to it.

It's only a matter of time. They'll come through that door, and he'll drop from up there.

Steven looked around the room, trying desperately not to give in to the franticness of the voice in his head.

Who knows how many of them there are. You're screwed.

Steven closed his eyes and leaned his head from side to side, stretching his neck. When he went to open his eyes again he found he couldn't, and a well of panic rose to the surface.

I told you, you're screwed.

Shutup.

Why don't you just give up?

I can't.

Come on, it would be so easy.

No.

Steven shut down that negative voice in his head, the one he thought he'd left behind long ago. The one that he'd shut down after his older brother died. Brian had always been his voice of reason, and when he'd died

Steven wanted to make sure that voice didn't die with him.

Steven backed himself up until he was against a wall.

At least no one can come from behind me.

He looked blindly around the room, trying to see with his mind's eye what the room looked like. The only door, six and a half feet in front of him. The grate he came through, slightly to the left and three feet away. The bed, sitting by the window two feet to the right of the door.

Relying on instinct alone he controlled his breathing, slowing it down, allowing as much oxygen into his brain as possible. When his mind was clear he concentrated on his heartbeat, taking control of the fear and adrenaline pumping through his body, he slowed it down to match his breathing. Even though he had been rendered blind and deaf, he could feel his mind taking on a heightened sense of its own. He could feel the dust falling through the air around him from where it had settled on the ductwork as the man who was after him crawled through its spaces.

He's close.

Steven rushed over to the bed, pushed it up against the door, and used the restraint straps to makeshift a temporary lock.

That should hold long enough to keep the others out while I deal with this guy.

Steven stepped carefully around the perimeter of the room, stopping when he came to the window. He turned to face it, resting his bloodied hand against the frame, and taking on a comfortable stance, as though he was simply watching his dog run around the backyard. His other hand, resting by his hip, danced slowly in the air keeping time with his heartbeat and breath. As the dust fell from the ceiling it gently flowed over to Steven's hand. Soon a pillar of dancing dust particles stood beside him.

Thump. Thump. Thump. Thump.

Four men. One would be too good to be true.

Steven knew he could talk, even if he couldn't hear himself.

"Four of you? Is that all the cavalry could afford?" He said, turning to face them.

The four men stood in a semicircle, deterred from immediate action by the sight in front of them. A ragged man, with one bloody hand, his eyes closed, and strangely calm.

"Well?" Steven asked tauntingly.

He felt one of the men take a step forward, and he ran at them. Flinging his right arm out, he sent the spiraling pillar of dust tornadoing towards them. All four men were incapacitated by the attack. They coughed and spluttered, tried to open their eyes, but it was all in vain.

Steven sprinted towards the man closest to the back wall of the room. Performing a parkour off of the wall, his right knee connected with the man's temple knocking him instantly unconscious. The echoes of the other men coughing bounced off the walls around him, and the vibration of an army running towards the room could be felt through the floor.

Steven grabbed the shoulders of the next man and dragged him over to the back wall, all while dodging the sporadic punches he was throwing. Steven threw him into the wall, and the man's head ricocheted off the wall. He looked stunned, as though a flash bang had gone off inside his skull, then dropped to the ground landing on his comrade's body. By this time the other two men had recovered, and were now advancing on Steven.

Steven took on a default defense stance; staggered legs with fists raised. One man approached from the left, the other from the right; he jumped for the man to the left. Steven's approach told the man he was going in for a head attack, and so he defended according to that, but at the last second Steven dropped to the ground and span, throwing his leg out, and kicking the man's feet out from underneath him. The man landed in a crumpled mess on the floor, and the hilt of his knife rammed into his solar plexus, winding him. Steven, still on the ground, flipped over to face the man to the right -who was already almost on top of him. He launched himself up off the ground with such power that when he flipped, his back landed against the chest of the man. Both men fell to the ground with Steven on top. He brought his knees down onto the man's arms, trapping him, and gave him one strong right hook that knocked him out.

A whoosh of air came towards the side of Steven's head and he ducked, barely dodging an attack from the man who'd been winded. Steven rolled forward towards the window, stood up and kept running as though he was going to dive out the window. He kicked himself off the window pane, splintering the glass, and launching his body over his attacker. Steven rolled into his landing, then rammed into the man faster than he could turn around. The man went flying forwards, catapulting through the window.

Steven breathed heavily, and he could feel the vibrations of the army on the other side of the door trying to break through. Suddenly the whole room began to shake, and sections of the concrete floor began rising up and down like crashing waves. The door finally flew open, sending the bed airborne. It crashed against the back wall and joined the motions of the floor, tumbling over broken chunks of concrete.

An emerald light, bright as the sun, flared into life at the same time as the door opened, and being unable to stay steady in a room that was falling apart Steven tumbled through the doorway.

He landed hard on the soft earth and grunted -he could hear it! Steven found he could open his eyes again also, and he looked up to see he was back in the glade. Sam, Kurtis and Lauren were already there, sitting in a small semicircle.

Hannah opened her eyes groggily. Bright lights flashed by overhead, and the feeling of shaky wheels vibrated beneath her. She could see Sam in her peripheral on another shaky wheeled bed beside her; her body bounced slightly signifying her unconsciousness. The voices around her were muffled, and as hard as she tried to listen the only word she managed to catch was 'swipe'.

Her heart lurched in her chest, she had to stop it from happening. Hannah tried to jump up off the bed, but her body wouldn't respond; the anesthesia had already done its job there. But she could use her mind.

Hannah dove into the depths of her brain, searching for the mental launch pad that would propel her into a cerebral connection with the doctors who were leading them to their fate. There it was, a glimmer of pale blue light. Hannah reached out for it and let it pull her along into the first doctor.

A junior who was helping wheel Sam along suddenly stopped in his tracks, his eyes went blank, and his arms flopped to his side.

"What is it?" One of the others asked.

When he didn't respond, the man who stood on the opposite side of Sam's bed slowly waved a hand in front of his face.

"Hello-o?"

Suddenly the junior's body twitched, and dropped to the floor.

"What the-"

The man who'd waved his hand was cut off as he went as slack-jawed as the junior was moments before. He similarly twitched, and dropped the floor. Quickly, panic spread among the four remaining, and they took off down the hall, leaving the girls behind.

Hannah leapt from doctor to doctor, chasing down that cerebral connection, shutting down their brains, thus causing a sudden unconsciousness to take over within them all. The length of the hall was the littered with the bodies of the doctors, and as the last one fell she snapped back into her own mind.

With an effort that annoyingly took more energy than the cerebral connections she'd just made, Hannah forced her hand up and over to Sam's, grabbing ahold of it, and squeezing tight. A warmth began to spread through her fingers, and when Hannah glanced down she could see a green light creeping through the edges of their hands. Wary at first she kept her hold on Sam's hand, but as the heat became unbearable she let go. A brilliantly blinding emerald light escaped from their hands, and suddenly the numbness in her body was no match for the need to cover her eyes. Hannah's arms flew up to her face, and she squinted as the green light slipped through the cracks.

Suddenly she felt herself drop, and everything disappeared. All that existed was herself, and the emerald light. Just when she thought she couldn't fall(or was she hovering) any longer it stopped, and there was ground beneath her. Hannah brought her arms down, and opened her eyes. Looking up there was a thick tree canopy, and as she rolled over she saw Sam sitting beside her; Lauren, Steven, and Kurtis next to her.

Chris' heart was pounding as he led them through the underground tunnels he'd found. He stopped to check their direction, to make sure he was leading them out, and not further in.

"Chris." There was a strain to Claire's voice, she was anxious.

"What's going on?" Kurtis asked.

A moment of silent tension hung in the air before Chris responded. "This way."

The three of them kept running. He was sure that at any moment they would hear feet chasing after them, feel the vibration of Grady's Authorities coming to take them back.

Soon they came to a split in the tunnel; one was fully built, and the other was still just a small opening.

"Come on." Chris whispered, ushering them through the small exit.

The sense that everything was about to horribly wrong struck Chris like a lightning bolt. He knew the next part of the story, and grabbed Claire's ankle, stopping her from continuing through.

What?! Claire's voice bounced around the inside of his skull, and the fear that powered it almost broke his heart.

Come back. Now.

But it was too late.

Chris and Kurtis stumbled at the sound of her scream, and as Kurtis pulled on his arm to lead them down the next tunnel the world around him froze. Chris wasn't going to stand by and watch this happen again.

Raising his arms up, and pulling them backward, like he was ripping something out of the air, Chris pulled down the wall of dirt that separated himself from Claire. Soil and rocks went flying around his body, rocketing down the tunnel they had just come from. Just inside the new room he was met with four men, armed to take him down. But just behind them, to where a man with striking red hair was dragging Claire away, was where his eyes had settled.

Chris took a step forward, and the four men began firing their weapons. Without wavering his gaze from Claire, Chris flicked his wrist, and the weapons came flying out of the men's hands. Their response was to run at him, but he had already turned the weapons on them, and fired. They dropped to the ground, their blood spilling and soaking into the soil.

Chris casually stepped over the felled bodies, walking with purpose towards the man who was dragging his sister away. As Chris made his first step onto the set of makeshift stairs, the man turned to face him, holding a gun up to Claire's head.

The only time he had seen this level of fear in his baby sister's eyes was when the flares had come, and he exploded. With the blink of an eye the gun fell to pieces and dropped to the ground. The man tightened his hold on Claire, wrapping one hand around her throat. Chris let out a rage-induced scream and jumped at the man. His large bicep flew just over Claire's head and crashed into the man's face. The man fell backward, his head bouncing off the top step, and sending him into a concussed sleep.

Claire clung to Chris, hugging him tightly, and crying into his back. Chris turned around, bringing an arm around his sister, and holding her close. The ground began to shake, and an emerald light exploded forth from the fissures in the soil. His arms collapsed into themselves as Claire was replaced by the same light, and Chris let out a scream of anguish. The light enveloped him, drowning out the sound of his scream. Then suddenly it was gone, and he was left standing in the glade with Kurtis beside him.

Kurtis could tell the simulation brought Claire back for him too, "Rough ride huh?"

Chris just slumped down against a tree beside him, tears blurring his vision. He tried to call out for her, but just as always there was no response.

Dean's eyelids flickered groggily. The world around him was a blur, and all he could sense was that he was lying on the ground. He could hear several voices talking amongst themselves, and he thought he could make out several faces staring down at him, but it all kept fading in and out as he slowly regained consciousness.

"Should we wake him?"

"What's going on?"

"I don't like this."

"Everybody shut up!"

"Well that's not very nice."

"Look, we can't just stand around. We have to do something."

"It's hopeless."

"Could you just try to be more positive."

"Hello?"

Dean groaned and rolled over, trying to ignore the voices. He slowly stood up, only to almost fall right back down. Darkness swam in his vision, and his head pounded. Someone grabbed his arm to help, but he waved them away, stumbling towards the back wall of the room.

I just need to sit.

Dean slid down the wall with a thump, one leg straight out, and the other bent up with his arm resting on the knee. He rubbed his eyes trying to clear them, and when he looked down at his hand his vision seemed to zoom in and out.

"Excuse me."

Dean looked up too quickly, and his hand grabbed at his head in response.

That face looks familiar...

"What's going on?" He managed to say.

"Well that's what we were hoping you could tell us, Boss."

"Boss?"

Even the voice sounds...

Dean looked into the man's face, and finally his vision focused. Being able to see it made him realize why everyone looked and sounded so familiar. Dean's eyes darted around the room, looking at the rest of the men with a sudden clarity. Dean was in a room with a bunch of Deans, all milling about looking lost.

Dean made to jump up, but Dean 2.0 put a hand on his shoulder, "You might want to stay seated for a bit. You were out for quite some time. We've been waiting for you."

"For what?"

"To put us back together, Boss."

"Stop calling me that."

Dean stood himself up slowly, using the wall to walk his hands up as support, and looked around. One Dean was crying in the corner, looking like a lost little boy. Another paced around the room impatiently as if he was about to go nuclear. Yet another sitting, seemingly staring off into space by a chess board. And one more huddled over in another corner of the room. All over the room Dean's were acting as if only one personality trait consumed his entire being.

"So, you're all... me?" Dean asked, as the two of him started walking around the room together.

"Five state-of-beings that have had a serious impact on your life, all separated and concentrated into one body." Dean 2.0 replied.

"What do you I call you?"

"Well, I am you."

"Okay... Dean. What do I do?"

"Oh, now that I can't tell you, Boss. None of us know how to fix this. You're the one with the fancy brain." Dean 2.0 tapped on Dean's head.

As they got closer to the one huddled in the corner Dean's face scrunched up in disgust at what he was doing.

"That one really wants to get back to Kaia." Dean 2.0 leaned over and whispered in Dean's ear matter-of-factly.

Dean shook his head and looked away, "Okay so, somehow I have to put myself back together again. I'll just start with something easy."

His gaze drifted back to the one pleasuring himself in the corner. Dean rolled his eyes and walked over to him.

Tapping him on the shoulder Dean said, "Hey there, um. How would you like to get back to your lovely wife? Maybe you could stop doing that, and enjoy the real thing."

"Sounds like a good deal to me."

"Just... stand still for a minute."

Dean went to the part of his brain that held his lust for Kaia, that animal part that took over in the heat of passion. It felt as though a piece of him was lost, which technically speaking it was considering his lust existed in a different body now. Dean located the empty space where it once resided, and started to spin the cerebral thread that would bring it back home.

Lustful-Dean started to waver, his body slowly fading from sight until all that was left was a pale blue light. The light floated towards Dean, and sank into his body.

"Well that's one down, only four left to go."

"Good job, Boss." Dean 2.0 said.

Dean just sighed, he had officially given up on asking his other self to stop calling him that. He scanned the room and looked at the others, then decided to go for the version of himself that had taken up to crying in the corner next.

"Alright kid, what's up?" He said as he squatted down, arms resting on either knee with his hands together.

"I want my mama." The Child-Dean sniffled.

Dean looked over to Dean 2.0 with an exasperated look.

"When you were young you were just a boy who wanted his mama."

That matter-of-fact tone wasn't helping, and Dean looked back to Child-Dean. He opened his mouth to speak, to try and comfort the boy, then he got an idea.

"If you come with me I can show you your mama."

Not a total lie, he had memories of her, he could show him that. Child-Dean sniffled again, his eyes were red and puffy from crying.

"You promise?" He wiped at his nose.

"I promise."

Child-Dean nodded, and he began the process again. Dean span the thread connecting that empty space to the Child-Dean in front of him, the blue light sank into his body, and he spasmed. Dean dropped to the floor, hands wrapped around his head, his mind felt like it was tearing itself apart.

"What's happening!?" Dean yelled.

"It appears as though the child in you is not pleased that you lied to him.

"How do you know I lied?" Dean grunted as another spasm shook his body.

Dean 2.0 didn't answer the question. Several minutes passed before the tremors finally stopped. Dean took a deep breath in and stood himself up.

"Alright, so no more white lies then. Who's next?"

"Might I suggest Logic next, I feel that Anger without it could spell trouble."

"Right." Dean said.

He walked over to the Dean sitting on a chair that faced a chess table, and took the seat opposite him. As he sat down he moved the queen's rook's pawn to A4.

"Hello Dean. I was wondering when we'd get to chat."

"Hello... " Dean trailed off, trying to think of something to call the man who sat in front of him.

"You can call me Mr. Whittaker, if it makes you feel more comfortable with the situation." He said, moving his king's pawn to E6.

"Alright then." Dean nodded his head, accepting the situation for what it was.

Dean hovered his hand above the board for a brief moment, then moved his king's rook's pawn up to H4.

"So Dean, what would you like to talk about?" Mr. Whittaker said, moving his king's bishop to B4.

"Well, I was hoping we could get back together. Ya know, leave this place and go save the world." Dean said, moving his king's knight to F3.

Mr. Whittaker moves his queen to F6 before replying, "And why would I want to do that?"

Dean's mind worked hard, playing a game of logic literally and metaphorically was daunting, especially with his logic sitting opposite him.

"I'm guessing you're not going to be convinced with 'because it's the right thing to do'." Dean said, settling on moving his king's rook to H3.

"Come, come, Dean. You should know better than that." Mr. Whittaker said, moving his queen's pawn to D5.

"You're right. Can't blame a guy for trying though." Dean said, moving his king's pawn to E3.

"Humor me Dean," Mr. Whittaker moved his king to F8, "Why do you even want to save the world? Is it really worth the trouble?"

Dean moved his king's knight to D4, putting it in the firing lane of Mr. Whittaker's queen.

"Trying to tempt me I see. It won't be that easy." He said moving his queen to H6.

"Have you ever been in love?"

Dean switched tactics, changing the subject, hoping it would throw him off enough to take control as he moved his king's bishop to C4.

Mr. Whittaker stalled a moment before responding, "I suppose I have been," He moved his queen's bishop to D7, "In love with the idea of love. It does seem fascinating."

Dean moved his king's pawn to E4. "It's a wonderful feeling, Mr. Whittaker, you really should try it some time."

"I've considered it, on its surface." He said, using his queen's pawn to take out Dean's king's pawn on E4. "But when you really get down to it, it seems far too dramatic. Sacrifices, liabilities, emotions. The mind was meant for much greater things."

"Sometimes sacrifices have to made, to make way for something greater." Dean moved his queen to G4, "It's always worth it."

"And sometimes it's misguided, and can get you into more trouble than it's worth." Mr. Whittaker moved his king's knight to F6.

Dean's queen was trapped, his only move was to retreat it back to E2.

Mr. Whittaker moved his queen's knight to A6.

Dean moved his king's rook to B3, forcing Mr. Whittaker to sacrifice his king's bishop or retreat; he chose the latter moving it back to D6.

"You know Dean, you've been a formidable opponent thus far, but you and I both know you can't keep this up forever."

Dean advanced his king's rook to B7, taking a pawn.

"You're right. So why don't you just give up now, rather than waste both of our time."

"So brash, what ever happened to the art of conversation." Mr. Whittaker chuckled and moved his queen's bishop to A4, taking a pawn.

Dean moved his king's knight's pawn up to G4, taunting Mr. Whittaker's king's knight at F6.

"Good, but not good enough." Mr. Whittaker said, seeing that taking to bait would lose him his king's knight, so he moved it to D7, taking it out of the line of fire.

Dean realized that the outcome of the game is what would win this, not words, and the more he concentrated on the game the closer he felt that cerebral thread to logic forming. He moved his queen's knight's pawn up to B3, trapping Mr. Whittaker's queen's bishop.

"Very clever." Mr. Whittaker paused before making a move for the first time since they had started. He settled for moving his king's bishop's pawn to F5.

Dean moved his queen's pawn to D3, putting Mr. Whittaker's queen's pawn in the same situation as his queen's bishop.

Mr. Whittaker settled on taking Dean's queen's pawn at D3; if he was going to lose it anyways he might as well take one of Dean's down with him.

Dean followed by capturing the pawn with his with his queen's bishop's pawn.

The speed and silence was starting to make Mr. Whittaker cocky, he didn't notice that he had his opening, his queen was set up perfectly to take Dean's queen's bishop and put him into checkmate. Missing this opportunity Mr. Whittaker made the move that would lead to his downfall. He moved his queen's knight to C5. Dean moved his Queen to F3. Mr. Whittaker moved his king's knight's pawn to G6.

The harder Dean concentrated the stronger the thread became, the stronger the thread became the more frantic Mr. Whittaker became.

Dean moved his king's knight to E6, capturing a pawn and directly threatening Mr. Whittaker's king. Mr. Whittaker twitched, his consciousness was slowly leaking back into Dean, and he was losing his grip.

Dean recognized what was happening, and turned his attention to locking Mr. Whittaker into that cerebral thread. Mr. Whittaker's body faded in and out, like static on a tv, one second he was a man, the next he was glowing figure of ethereal blue light.

"Gotcha." Dean whispered as he made the connection complete.

Mr. Whittaker's blue light engulfed Dean, sinking into his body until he sat there shaking. The effort of slowly piecing himself back together was beginning to take a toll on him.

"Good job, Boss."

"Yeah." Dean nodded, glancing at the walking rage machine wearing his face.

"One more thing, Boss."

"What is it?"

"You may want to be careful with this one, and be ready to take me on as soon as you've conquered him."

"I'll have to absorb him, and immediately take you afterward?"

"Yes, and I'll be ready for that. Calm, and ready." Dean 2.0 was putting an emphasis on the word 'calm'.

"What if it I can't keep it in check?"

"I have faith in you, Boss. Just remember to have faith in yourself." Dean 2.0 smiled at him.

Dean raised his eyebrows at him, and looked back over to his anger, waving at him as their eyes met.

"How's it going?" Dean asked casually.

"What do you want?" Rage-Dean asked.

"Alright then, right to it. Well, I kind of need you to get back in my head. You know, so we can all leave. Go home. Kill the bad guy. Save the world."

Rage-Dean stopped pacing, "You've found Grady?"

"Not yet. We're working on it. We're trying to stop his biomechanical army first."

Rage-Dean averted his gaze downwards, and spoke aloud to himself.

"It would give us time to practice.", "Vengeance on Grady.", "Killing along the way.", "Could be fun.", "I like it."

"Let's go." He said, looking up at Dean.

"Awesome." Dean said.

He placed a hand on the man's shoulder, and shuddered at the intensity of the rage he felt emanating from him.

He was disgusted that a part of him had the potential to be like this. It reminded him of how angry he'd been in his years at the facility before he'd met Kaia.

"Here goes." Dean whispered to himself preparing for the worst, and made the connection.

Rage-Dean exploded into a bright light, starting out blue just like the others, but quickly flickering into a deep red. The light dove into Dean's body sending him flying backward, and knocking the wind out of him.

"Boss!" Dean 2.0 yelled, running after Dean's ragdolled body.

Dean began to spasm as Dean 2.0 slid to his knees beside him, grabbed his shoulders, and held on as tight as he could.

"You can do this, Boss! Look for your Calm! Make the connection. I've got you."

Dean struggled in his head, it felt like he was drowning. He tried to find Calm, he was desperate for it, but struggling to fight above the rage was chaos in itself.

Suddenly he could feel Dean 2.0 grabbing ahold of him, could hear his voice. Dean used the physical connection to anchor him, to find his Calm.

Just remember to have faith in yourself.

He'd found it, the cerebral thread that would bring Calm back into his world and save his life. He raced down the thread, Rage-Dean close behind. The effort burned his lungs as he pushed himself twice as hard.

"I've got you, Boss."

Then suddenly the connection was made. Calm came rushing forward, enveloping Dean and quelling Rage in an intense blue light.

Dean's eyes opened wide, and he almost cried at the feeling of pure serenity that flowed through his body in that moment. Just as the intensity died he heard a final whisper.

Hold on to something, Boss, it's about to get rough.

Dean jumped up and looked around. The seams in the walls began to crack, the floor rumbled, and the ceiling started to shake. Chunks of plaster fell to the ground as the room disintegrated, and the gaping holes were replaced with a beautiful emerald light. Dean caught himself staring into the light when a piece of the ground beneath him lurched upwards and knocked him off balance. Dean jumped from piece to piece, dodging chunks of ceiling as they came crashing down. One of the walls fell down in one piece forming a makeshift slide, and he dove for it. He landed with both feet, sliding down easily until a blast of emerald light caused him to throw his arms up to protect his eyes. As the light dissipated he brought his arms down, and he realized he was back in the forest glade, everyone sitting around him. Everyone except Kaia. Dean looked around at the balls of emerald light, one of which was brighter than the rest. He gravitated towards it, staring into the depths of the light.

"She's the only one who hasn't come out yet." Lauren said, walking up behind him, and placing a hand on his shoulder. Dean jumped a little at the contact.

"Don't worry, she'll be fine. She's a tough one." Lauren tried to comfort him.

"I know. " Dean said, but he couldn't help worrying.

Kaia woke up tied to a chair at the end of a hallway. She looked around, recognizing the situation as a recurring nightmare she'd had as a teenager. Kaia worked her fingers up underneath the rope, slowly loosening it. As she expected a buzzing sound started and a purple light flared into existence and the end of the hallway. One line of purple light ran across the room at shin height, and another at neck height.

Lasers.

They made their way towards Kaia, and she pulled harder against the ropes, wriggling her fingers into the knot.

Come on.

The lasers had made it almost all the way to her.

Got it.

The rope fell from her wrists just in time, and she jumped off the chair diving through the opening between the lasers. The tips of her hair crossed through one of them and turned to ash. Kaia quickly put her hair up in a bun and waited for whatever came next. Bright purple lines that ran from the floor to the ceiling started flying past her, and she dodged them all. Dipping, jumping, and swirling just in time.

The next pattern of laser beams came at her like a lattice fence, the only opening was a foot of space at the top-this was when she usually died and woke up in a sweat, but not this time. She spotted a ventilation grate in the ceiling between her and the advancing laser beams. Kaia sprinted towards the grate and jumped up, grabbing it seconds before the lasers reached her. She pulled herself up, pinning her body along the ceiling while the lasers passed under her. Kaia let go, landing in a squatted position. She glanced behind her just in time to see the lasers vanish on the other side. A panel in the far wall opened up, and she walked through it. As she emerged on the other side it slid back into place and disappeared, as if it was never there.

Kaia's footsteps echoed as she walked into the circular room before her. Various weapons hung from the walls: large two-handed axes, stiletto daggers, flails of various shapes and sizes, sickles, spears, ornate fighting gloves that made each knuckle into a small blade or spike, and forearm blades.

Kaia picked up one of the blades and strapped it to her arm with one buckle by the elbow and another above the wrist. There was a handle to hold onto to maintain control of the long blade the protruded from it, as well as a shorter blade that jutted out behind the elbow.

A girl could get used to this.

Although I am glad I still have this...

She looked down at her Glock, held firmly in place against her ribs in its holster.

Kaia heard someone enter the room, and she quickly looked up aiming her firearm at the intruder, the blade at her side.

"Who are you?" She asked, but she got no response.

The shadowed figure advanced into the room until they were equally as far from the center as Kaia was.

"I said, who are you?" She took a step forward, her senses alert and ready to fight.

The figure threw his head back, and cast the shadow away, to reveal Grady standing there. Kaia smirked, thankful that the simulation had given her the opportunity to really let off some steam.

The Grady look alike grinned, his eyes flashed pure black, and he shimmered a little bit.

Just as Kaia went to fire at him, he multiplied, and suddenly she was surrounded by six Gradys.

Conjurings...

"That's a clever trick you got there." Her smile turned to something fiercer, "Come get some."

They all ran at her, and she sprinted for the one closest to her, driving her blade into his chest. Blood gurgled out of his mouth, and she placed a boot against his stomach kicking him off the blade. One of them was right behind her, and as the blade slid free of the other one's chest she drove her elbow up and backward. The smaller blade landed in the new one's eye. He screamed and grabbed at his face, blood pouring out of his ruptured eye socket. Kaia fired a bullet into the head of the man she had skewered through the chest, then another into the head of the one she had visually impaired.

Kaia turned to face the other four, and emptied the rest of her magazine into them. The other three conjurings suffered fatal shots while the real(simulated) one dodged them with ease.

When her gun was emptied he walked around the perimeter of the room, slowly, like he was toying with her. Kaia took the opportunity to reload her gun and take off the arm blade, which she tossed aside; the clatter echoing through the room.

Grady began conjuring up some more, and Kaia knew what she had to do. Soon the room was full of Gradys and Kaias, all ready to fight to the death. Everyone grabbed the weapons off the walls and ran at each other; the fighting was bloody and brutal.

One Kaia had donned a pair of the ornate fighting gloves, and was punching her way through as many Gradys as she could. Each Grady she left behind was unrecognizable, faces pulverized into mangled flesh, bodies twitching as they choked on their own blood. Another wielded a large axe, chopping the arms and legs off her enemies. Blood arced through the air, and splattered across everyone within range.

Gradys wielding sickles, driving them into the abdomens of Kaias, lifting their bodies into the air and ripping them apart, showering blood and innards upon themselves.

Other Gradys were fighting off stiletto dagger wielding Kaias with various flails. One Kaia would dodge the flail and rise up just in time to drive her weapon up under a Gradys rib cage, while another wouldn't jump back in time and would get her face shattered by the heavy bladed ball of the deadly weapon.

It was pure carnage.

Kaia picked up a spear off the wall and looked around the room, looking for the right one. The conjurings were good but they weren't perfect, the real one would have a telltale sign, just as she did: the movements, the reaction time, the instinct.

There.

Grady was smiling wickedly, watching as the slaughter unfolded. Kaia kept her spear low, waiting for the opportune moment to strike. He was distracted, but not enough. Kaia dove into the fray, one eye on Grady the entire time. She drove her spear through a line of Gradys, and as she ripped it free they fell to the ground clutching their destroyed bellies.

Now.

Kaia threw the spear through the air, and it thudded into Grady's chest.

All of his conjurings stopped in their tracks, turning to static, flashing in and out of existence as blood bubbled out of Grady's mouth. Kaia made a beeline for him, emptying her clip into his torso as she approached him. Grady was on his knees in front of her, bullet holes oozing blood, spear protruding from his sternum. Kaia gripped the spear and ripped it upwards, slicing open his throat in the process. He fell down face first into his own puddle of blood.

Kaia looked around the room, blinking the sweat out of her eyes. The conjurings all faded, and she was left alone standing in a blood-bath. Suddenly the room was filled with a bright emerald light, soft at first, then all too suddenly, brilliantly blinding. Kaia covered her eyes, waiting for the light to die. The emerald light flared one last time, and when she opened her eyes again she was standing back in the forest glade with Dean's arms wrapped around her.

When Dean finally let her go she pointed the remote upwards, turning the simulation off, and bringing the environment back to the domed metal room. The distinct ringing of alarms could be heard now that the simulation program was off, and it was one they'd hoped they'd never hear.

"What's going on?" Steven asked.

"There's been a breach at the entrance." Kaia said, running out the door.

Chapter 20

The group sprinted through halls and rooms, the sounds of the attack getting louder with every turn they made. The set of doors leading to the entrance opened to reveal Ben and Freddie leading a retaliation on the Hunter that was forcing itself into their base. Jack, Amara, Gerard, Ki, and Sasha were with them, along with several soldiers.

"What happened?!?" Dean shouted above the gunfire, taking up position by Ben.

"It just ripped the door off! Usually they just collide with it then leave. I don't know-"

Kaia had stopped in her tracks, unnoticed by the rest of the group, as if in a trance.

Wires dangling. Flickering lights. Blood.

Kaia blinked, trying to focus.

Dean, impaled. Dead. Hannah, bloody. Dead. Ben, legs gone. Dead. Everyone. Dead.

The coppery smell of blood filled her nose, and she started to panic. Time, for Kaia, slowed down to a near halt. Her vision was coming to life, and her mind couldn't take it.

Kaia!!

Dean's voice broke the barrier, and suddenly everything unfroze, and she was back in the game. She pulled her Glock out of its holster, and fired into the screaming face of a Hunter as it broke through, but the bullets seemed to just get swallowed by its bulbous flesh, and it kept coming.

She joined the line of soldiers, and eventually the Hunter backed away, using half of its limbs to cover its oozing face, and the others to drag itself backward.

Jack high-fived Ki, Amara sighed, and Gerard and Sasha laughed jovially at one another. But behind all that, an eerie silence hung over them.

"It's not over yet." Kaia said, gloom shrouding her voice.

A loud creak resonated throughout the building, starting above their heads, and stretching down the hallway. Everyone looked, following the sound with their eyes.

"Everyone up against the walls, now."

Dean ushered everyone out of the middle of the hallway turned battle arena, backs to the walls, and weapons aimed at the torn up entrance. There was a moment of silence, then it all happened at once.

Metal appendages tore through the ceiling, and grabbed at whoever they could reach, dragging bodies through the shredded metal remnants of the roof; the screams as their limbs would get caught and rip free were blood-curdling. Soldiers dodged the falling limbs only to slip in blood on their next step, but they kept firing.

Jack was setting up a large Railgun at the end of the hallway, preparing for the inevitable breakthrough. Dean was being pushed closer and closer to the floor as he emptied the clip of an AK-47 into the mouth of a Hunter that was about to bite his head off. It screamed and retreated back outside, only to be replaced by two more trying to squirm their way in. Dean rolled out of the way and yelled to Jack, "How much longer til that thing's ready to go!?"

Just as Jack opened his mouth to reply a chunk of ceiling collapsed to the floor, making a ramp up to the opening in the roof. Kaia caught Sam and Hannah out of the corner of her eye just as they disappeared up and out.

Lauren, cover me!

Kaia sprinted for the ramp, dodging the Hunters' attacks as they tried to skewer her with their mechanized limbs. Lauren shot at them as they came down, throwing the Hunters off balance and averting their aim. Once Kaia was out of sight she dove under the ramp taking cover.

"Ready!" Jack yelled.

Up on the roof Sam had jumped on top of a Hunter, and was ramming her knife into the joints where its flesh joined with metal. It was thrashing about, trying desperately to throw her off, but she held on tight. Hannah was weaving in between and around the limbs of another one, using a rope to wrap around them. She gave the rope one final tug and the Hunter toppled over, falling through the now gaping hole in the roof. They could hear the bang as Jack launched a projectile at it, and the flames from it shot up through the opening. The Hunter Sam was on top of reeled backward from the heat, and she went flying onto the ground below.

"Sam!!" Hannah screamed, running to the edge of the roof.

Sam waved up at her, grunting as she pulled herself up.

Kaia pulled out her Ithaca 37, and started pumping shots into the Hunter, forcing it to back up towards the hole in the roof.

Dean, get ready. Here comes another.

The group below could see the first limb come scraping into view. Kaia had to stop to reload, and it disappeared from view again.

Kaia. What's going on?

She didn't respond, focusing solely on reloading as fast as possible.

Kaia!?

Just as the Hunter was about to impale Kaia she raised her weapon and fired a shot right into the joint of the limb that was coming for her. It blew off and slid down the ramp. The Hunter screeched and stumbled, trying to regain its balance. Kaia pumped the rest of her shots into it, and it toppled down the ramp.

Jack fired the railgun again, and again flames shot up out of the hole. Kaia dove out of the way, covering her head, to avoid the blast of heat.

Sam ran to the front of the base and tried to climb back through the wreckage of the front door, but the electricity that sparked every other second made it near impossible. Sam looked behind her to see five more of Grady's Hunters coming at them.

"Shit." She said to herself.

Hannah, while staying on the roof, had followed Sam around to the front of the building, and what she saw terrified her. Hannah reached inside herself, ignoring the fear, and tapped into her abilities. Everything in her wanted to rip apart the machines that were going to kill the woman she loved, and she drew on that.

Meanwhile, Sam pulled four shock grenades out of her belt and pulled the pins on them. She held onto them, knowing they wouldn't go off until an impact was made, waiting to throw them until the Hunters were closer.

Kaia looked up to see Hannah standing near the front of the building, but couldn't tell what was happening.

Hannah?

When she didn't respond, Kaia moved towards her.

Sam tossed her grenades, then pulled out a Calico 960 SMG. Electricity sparked and danced across the five Hunters, and a barrage of bullets hammered into them, but all it did was slow them down. Knowing she was a goner she reached out to Hannah.

I'm sorry Hannah, I love you.

She heard a scream from above, and at the same time the five Hunters blew apart. All of their mechanical parts were torn from them, and the lumps of flesh that remained fell to the ground with a wet splat, all snarling and snapping.

Just as Kaia reached Hannah she fell down, heading for the ground below. Kaia grabbed Hannah's hand and pulled her back just in time, her body falling limply into her arms.

Dean. It's over. We're safe for now. Shut down the power so Sam can get through the door.

Moments later an alarm bell rang, and the electricity sparks ceased. Sam saw Kaia pulled Hannah's body back from the edge of the building, and knew something was wrong. Kaia looked down at Hannah with tears in her eyes, at a loss for what to do. She was dying.

"I'm-" Hannah coughed up blood, "I'm sorry. Tell-" She coughed again.

"Sh, sh, sh. You can tell her yourself okay. Come on girl." Kaia smiled through her tears, trying to reassure her.

Kaia repositioned Hannah in her arms and walked back to the ramp.

Hannah, bloody. Dead.

Sam made her way through the busted doorway and ran to the ramp, meeting Kaia halfway, and taking on some of Hannah's weight. The weight shift instigated a fresh coughing fit from Hannah, and blood sprayed out of her mouth. When the coughing subsided she spat a glob of blood onto the ground.

"Just put me down." Hannah whispered.

They slid her to the ground, leaning her up against a wall so she was in a seated position. Sam knelt down at her side and took Hannah's face in her hands.

"Why did you do that?"

"I couldn't-" She coughed again, and Sam wiped the blood from her mouth, "I couldn't let you die. I love you."

Sam couldn't hold the tears back that were blurring eyes anymore.

"No, no, no. Don't you say your goodbyes. Hannah!"

Sam pulled Hannah's body closer to hers, and her head flopped to the side.

"Hannah!"

Sam's body heaved with the power of her sadness and anger. She rocked back and forth, holding Hannah to her, crying into her shoulder. Everyone stood around the two, tears falling, hands to mouths, helpless to do anything.

Kaia knelt down beside her friend, gently placing a hand on her shoulder. Sam twitched with the contact, and looked up into Kaia's eyes.

"Let me help you."

Sam nodded hopelessly, silent tears still running down her face. The women picked up Hannah's body, and left.

Dean, you should stay and make sure repairs are done on this. We can't risk anything else getting in. Kaia's voice was solemn as she spoke to him.

Of course.

Dean watched them carry Hannah's body away until they were completely out of view.

Chapter 21

"Colonels, Captains, take the soldiers to The Lab and get yourselves patched up. Lauren, Steven, Chris, Kurtis, stay here." Dean said.

Jack nodded, and each superior officer helped to carry an injured soldier while trying not to look into the faces of the ones they'd lost. Once they were gone Dean turned to those he'd asked to stay.

"Okay guys, I want to try something, a test run if you will. I wish we'd have had time to discuss what we all experienced in the simulation room but we didn't."

"What do you want to do?" Steven asked.

"I want everyone to tap into their telekinesis. Remember what this place looked like before this happened." Dean walked around, kicking chunks of rubble out of the way. "Because whatever makeshift repair we could whip up, wouldn't hold for long anyways."

"Alright. Let's do this then." Chris said, stepping up the ruins of the main entrance.

Everyone stepped up beside him, and all at once they dove into their psyche -each of them picturing what the area looked like prior to the attack in their mind's eye. A rumble soon emanated from the beneath them as their collective power vibrated through the ruined materials, and things started to move. Wires pulled themselves back together, small pieces of rubble rolled over to larger portions, and slowly but surely the entryway was rebuilding itself. Soon the process sped up: the makeshift ramp flew back up to the ceiling, the main door snapped back into place, and within a few minutes it looked as though nothing had happened -aside from the dead bodies that were strewn about the hall.

"That. Was. Awesome." Steven said.

"Alright everyone, get some rest, and we'll see you in the morning." Dean nodded at them and left.

"So, what do you think about all this?" Kurtis asked around a mouthful of mashed potatoes and veggies.

"Dude. Chew with your mouth closed." Chris said, using his fork to fling a pea at Kurtis.

Kurtis flipped him the bird, and caught the pea in his mouth. The two chuckled, but it was short-lived.

"Seriously though. A few days ago we were just a couple of ordinary soldiers."

"We were never exactly, 'ordinary'" Chris said, referring to their innate ability to communicate within each other's minds.

"Stop being so melodramatic." Kurtis took a big gulp of water and pushed away his empty plate.

"You're right, it's just..."

"I know man. We'll get her out." Kurtis leaned forward across the table. "I won't stop until she's back. You know that. And now it seems we have an upper hand in all of this. So cheer up a little would you. There's no use sulking. Claire is a tough girl, she can handle whatever they throw at her."

"You're right." Chris sighed and stood up, leaving the dining hall.

"Where are you going?" Kurtis asked.

"For a run." And with that Chris started jogging down the hallway towards the gym.

Kurtis ran a hand through his hair sighing, then headed for his room.

Steven and Lauren lay entangled in each other's bodies, the sheets were wet with sweat, and the blanket was tossed to the ground. Lauren's hand dropped the ground and pulled it back up over their legs.

"It's been nice having our own bed." Steven said, his fingers running up and down Lauren's arm.

"Yeah. Is it weird that there's a part of me that misses sneaking around in the middle of the night to get to you for our late night rendezvous'." She said, laughing a little.

"Only a little." Steven said.

When all that could be heard was their breathing Lauren's mind drifted to what had happened earlier.

"I can't believe Hannah's dead. She was such a sweet woman. And Sam..."

"She must be a wreck."

"I'm glad Kaia is with her. I couldn't bear the thought of her being alone right now."

Dean wanted to go and see Kaia, to see how Sam was doing, but he had a detour to make first. He knocked on a door in the barracks halls, and a man answered.

"General Whittaker." He yawned, "What can I do for you?"

"There was a... well for lack of better words, an incident at the main entrance. I'm sorry to bother you so late, but it's a big job, and I don't want there to be a panic when the night crew return in the morning."

"How big are we talking?"

"There was a break in. Everything's fine, there's just..."

"A body count."

"Yeah..."

"I'm on it."

"Thanks."

The man started rummaging through a closet, bring out various cleaning supplies and a pair of ragged overalls.

"And James."

"Yeah?"

"We will win. I promise."

James nodded with a forced smile on his face, then ducked back into the closet while Dean took his leave.

Sam and Kaia carried Hannah in silence, all the way to the final elevator. It took them to the subbasement, where The Graveyard was. It was a place that served as a safe place to bury their dead. A place that people could visit, and a place where people knew their loved ones wouldn't be disturbed by war anymore. Kaia knew that Sam would want to do this herself, so she dismissed Gregory as he approached, and the two women began to dig.

Dean approached the double doors that led to The Graveyard and stopped just outside, one palm against them.

Kaia?

Yes?

How's she doing?

Kaia looked up from her digging and glanced at Sam's face. Tears still trickled from her bloodshot eyes.

How would you be doing? Kaia responded.

Dean nodded. *Do you want some help?*

Yes. But not in here.

Where?

Go and talk to Ed. See how they're doing with the triangulation devices. Sam's going to be looking for blood soon, and I want to make sure we're ready to go.

Alright. ... I love you.

Love you too.

Knock. Knock. Knock.

Ed grumbled and rolled over in his bed pulling the blanket over his head.

Knock. Knock. Knock.

Ed lifted his wrist and squinted. His watch read 12:07 am.

Knock. Knock. Knock.

"Alright, alright. I'm coming, I'm coming."

Ed sat up and yawned, stretching as he reached for his robe. He opened the door, eyes still adjusting to the light, and barely managed to distinguish the silhouette of a well-built man entering his small room.

"Come on in." He said sarcastically.

"How's the emp plan coming?"

Ed rubbed the sleep out of his eyes, and looked towards the voice.

"General Whittaker?"

Dean took a seat at Ed's breakfast table, "One of them, yes."

Ed just blinked at him, still waking up.

"Now, how's the emp plan coming along?" Dean asked.

Ed cleared his throat, turned on a lamp, then took the other seat at the table. "We were going to start running preliminary tests tomorrow. We have the equipment ready, we just want to be sure of the results."

"Thank you. Will you wait to run them until we get there?"

"Yes, of course. What's with the sudden urgency though? I mean I know it's urgent. But it seems... more so now."

Dean paused before replying. "We'll talk tomorrow."

Before Ed could say anymore Dean left, leaving him to flop back down onto his bed. Groaning he threw an arm over his eyes and drifted back to sleep.

The hole was dug, and Hannah's body lay peacefully beside it. Kaia stood by Sam, waiting for her to speak first. Minutes of silence passed before she finally did speak.

"Why did she do it?" Sam said, her voice hoarse from dehydration.

Sam looked up at Kaia, and repeated the question, "Why?"

There was no answer to the question other than 'because she loved you', so Kaia sent as much emotion out to Sam as she could. Sympathy, love, comfort.

"Why didn't you stop her!?"

Sam was angry.

Kaia knew it wasn't at her, and she replied calmly. "By the time I realized what was happening it was too late. I'm sorry. I-"

"Sorry doesn't bring her back does it!?" Sam had gotten right in Kaia's face at this point.

"You're right Sam. But that's all I can say. I'm so sorry this happened to you, and to her. It's not fair."

Sam's face seethed with anger, and then she broke, crumpling into Kaia's arms and crying. Kaia stroked her hair and held her close, continuing to pour emotional support into her mind. Sam finally looked up and wiped her tears with the sleeve of her shirt, then turned to look at Hannah's body. She squatted down beside her and pulled the wedding band off her heart-finger.

"We never actually got married. But we had it all planned out. You know, for when we finally defeated the creatures. Hah. Grady's Hunters. Fuckin' prick."

Sam said, sliding Hannah's ring onto a chain that hung from her neck.

"She loved you very much." Kaia said, putting a hand on Sam's shoulder.

Sam nodded, sighed, then placed her hands under Hannah's shoulders; she was ready. Kaia picked up her feet, and they gently placed Hannah in the ground.

They continued the rest of her burial in silence.

Kaia opened the door to her room quietly, and climbed into bed. She was slightly startled when Dean pulled her in close, she'd expected he'd be asleep by now.

"You didn't have to wait up for me." Kaia said.

"I know I didn't have to. I wanted to."

He kissed her forehead, and she smiled.

"We patched up the entrance. Looks good as new."

"Really?" Kaia asked, turning around in his arms to get comfortable.

"Yeah, we all pulled together and tapped into the telekinesis. It was kind of awesome."

"That's... well awesome." Kaia chuckled, "What did you find out from Ed?"

"He's ready to start running tests on the equipment tomorrow. I told him to wait for us to arrive to start them."

"Perfect." Kaia's eyes closed, and she started to drift off.

"And Sam?" Dean asked.

"She wanted to be left alone for a while."

Sam sat beside Hannah's grave, tears blurring her vision as she stared at the fresh mound of dirt; the only indication of a body there.

"Can I get you anything miss?"

Sam looked up, bringing her sleeves -already stained with wetness- up to her eyes to catch the tears. "No, thank you Gregory I- ... Actually, can you get me something to mark the grave with? Something simple." Sam gazed into the distance, a gentle smile forming on her face, "Hannah always wanted something simple."

Gregory had a feeling she was talking about more than just the grave marker. "Of course."

He returned a short moment later with two thick wooden sticks and some white twine.

"Thank you."

Sam pulled a small switchblade from her boot, picked up the shorter stick, and started carving into it.

Chapter 22

Sam stood in the corner of the room, her eyes downcast and grey from a night of no sleep. All around her men and women were mustering the courage for another day out on the field, and as she listened to the Generals speak it all began to blur, and their voices became muffled as they floated past her ears. It was everyone's footsteps marching out of the room and into imminent danger that eventually brought her back to reality. Sam looked up as the last of them trailed out. It was just Kaia, Dean, Lauren, Steven, Chris, Kurtis and herself left in the room.

"Okay. we're gonna walk and talk." Kaia said as she moved towards the doorway. "Dean told me how you guys repaired the entrance way after the attack last night. That's incredible, but we're still all going to have to put as much time as possible into that simulation room as we can in the time that we have. Right now though we're going to see Ed and his team of techs."

Kaia swiped her I.D badge on a panel, opening the door leading to the next section of the base.

"Dean spoke with Ed last night, and they are ready to run preliminary tests on the equipment we will be using to incapacitate Grady's Hunters."

Kaia swiped her badge again for another door to reveal a few men, Ed and Gi among them, sitting around a cluttered workspace.

"I don't know how you guys get anything done." Kaia said, humor in her voice.

"It's an organized mess." Ed said, lifting a mask from his eyes, and putting down a soldering gun. His face read confusion when he saw the entourage Kaia had brought with her.

"They're all a part of this."

"Of course, I just wasn't expecting so many people." Ed cleared his throat, and pushed his chair away from the desk standing up, "Follow me then."

Ed, along with Gi and two other techs, led them down a set of stairs to a large room occupied by an equally large table with legs that held it up at mid-chest height. As each person entered they took a place around the table, and when all was quiet Ed flipped the lights off and pressed a large blue button. A hologram shot up from the table displaying a replica of the environment surrounding the base. At the top two corners and bottom center of the table sat three identical devices.

"These three pieces of equipment," Ed said while pointing at them, "are what you will use to perform the triangulation emp to shut these creatures-"

"Hunters." Dean said.

"Hunters," Ed nodded at him, "down. I don't know how much the devices can take on at once, so I'm going to run several scenarios with various numbers of Hunters within range."

He stood for a moment, looking around awkwardly before opening a tray at the end of the table he stood at. A complicated looking keyboard ejected from the table, and he tapped away on it. Ten holographic Hunters appeared in the open field.

"Here goes." He said.

Ed and the two other techs flipped a small switch on the underside of the three devices, and almost immediately the ten Hunters spasmed and fell to the ground motionless.

"It works." Ed breathed, his eyes lighting up in excitement.

He tapped away at the keyboard again, and those ten were replaced by twenty-five fresh ones, who were in turn incapacitated just like the others. Ed repeated the test over and over until the table was crawling with holographic Hunters.

Finally the devices reached their limit.

"Two hundred." Kaia said.

"Two hundred." Ed repeated back to her.

"That'll work." She said, "Keep them here and ready to go."

"Can do."

Kaia led her group up and out of the room.

Once they were out and walking Kaia spoke again, "I'm going to see Dr. Lee now to get an update on the status of the bait. I want to be able run this mission as soon as possible. In the meantime you should head to the simulation room and get in some more training. A-button for single training like last time, B-button for group training, C-button cycles through environs. I'll join you later."

Steven, Lauren, Chris, Kurtis, and Sam broke off, heading for the simulation room, while Dean followed Kaia to Dr. Lee.

"Do you think we're ready for this." Dean asked.

"We have to be." Kaia said.

There was something hard about her expression, like determination, but darker.

Dean grabbed her shoulders, and stopped in front of her. "We still have to be careful."

"I know." She said, "I know." Softer this time.

Sam had slipped away from the group the first chance she got, and headed for the weapons room; she needed to get out.

Where are you going?

Out.

You're going to get yourself killed.

Yeah well...

Well what?

"You're not actually here. I'm just talking to myself." Sam said.

But Hannah's voice persisted to be in her head.

I am here. Stay with me.

Sam screamed, throwing a box of ammo against the wall.

Hannah's voice stopped.

Sam continued strapping various weapons and holsters to her body until she looked like a one-woman-army, then headed outside.

Kaia and Dean looked at the lump of flesh sitting on the operating table.

"So the code definitely works then." Kaia said, lifting one of its eyelids open. It snapped shut as soon as she let it go.

"Yes it does." Seong hooked her finger under and into a small flap of skin located on the underside of the creature's mouth. A small keyboard with ten buttons popped out.

"This is where you will input the code once they are down." Seong said, handing Kaia a piece of paper.

"This is it, make sure everyone who is going out there knows it."

"Thank you." Kaia said, putting the paper in her back pocket.

"The chips are implanted, and will be activated as soon as you're ready to take it outside." Seong said.

"Sounds good. We'll be ready in two weeks." Kaia said.

They left, heading for the simulation room. When they arrived the door was locked, indicating an active session, so they sat and waited for the group to emerge.

Chapter 23

Sam had run through squads of soldiers, past battles, and through great tree corpses until she reached a hill. It seemed strange to be where it was, but it was one of the only spots still left with grass on it. It was patchy and brown, but it was there.

She'd come here with Hannah to break for a quick drink or meal while out on the field often, but today she came here alone. Sam ran up the small hill, sat down, and cried. When the sobs no longer wracked her body she conjured up a scene.

Beautiful green grass covered the little hill, and a great willow tree shaded it. Rays of sun burst through the leaves, and a gentle breeze rustled the hanging branches. Hannah stood there with her hand held out, and her face shining with love. Her long blonde hair was down, and beautifully curled with silver flowers weaved throughout it. She wore an elegantly simple white dress with thin straps and a flowing skirt.

Sam smiled, and the tears slowed to a trickle. She held her hand out, as though reaching for Hannah's, and watched as a conjuring of herself walked towards Hannah.

She wore a similar dress, but hers had a long black ribbon tied just under the bust, and where the ribbon came together at the back was a large bow.

A voice emanated from where the tree stood, but there was no one else around. "Do you, Hannah Adler, take Samantha Darkholme to be your lawfully wedded wife?"

"I do."

"And do you, Samantha Darkholme, take Hannah Adler to be your lawfully wedded wife?"

Just as Sam whispered 'I do', a long mechanical limb swiped through the conjuring, ending it abruptly. Sam jumped up, pulling the pins three grenades, and tossed them into the Hunter's screaming mouth. They exploded immediately, and the Hunter's head blew open sending chunks of flesh and metal all over the hill.

Everyone emerged from the room, smiling and laughing. Clearly the simulation had gone well, but their smiles were cut short when they saw the look on Kaia's face.

"What's wrong?" Lauren asked.

"Where's Sam?"

"She's right-"

Lauren turned, intending to point at Sam, and just as she did Sam wavered and disappeared. A conjuring.

"Shit." Kaia said, then ran for the weapons room. The others quickly followed.

Kaia geared up as fast as she could, everyone else following suit.

"What do you think happened?" Chris asked.

"That she's gone out on some reckless blood hunt." Kaia said.

"Why would she-" Lauren started.

"To blow off steam. Revenge. Either way, she's not thinking straight. And although there's a crew out there right now, I'm willing to bet she's not with them."

Kaia loaded a magazine into her Glock and thrust it into its holster.

"Couldn't we just try to reach out to her from here? Talk her into coming back?" Steven asked.

"We could, but it's doubtful she'd listen. We need to find her, bring her back to her senses. And that's easier to do up close than far away." Kaia tossed her Ithaca over her shoulder. "When we go out there, we stick together. Leave it to me to contact her. Too many voices in her head could just distract her, and she could wind up dead." Kaia paused for a moment, the image of Hannah falling flashed through her mind. "And please be careful. Don't push your limits."

Are you okay? Dean asked.

Kaia flashed him a reassuring smile.

"Let's go." Kaia said.

The group jogged through the hallways, their gear clunking against their bodies with each step.

Ben and Freddie were standing guard, as usual.

"Good afternoon. I wasn't expecting to see you heading out today." Ben said, looking at Kaia and Dean.

"Did you see Sam leave?" Kaia asked.

"Yeah, about three or four hours ago. Why?"

Before Kaia could respond there was a knock on the door. Freddie went to The Pipe and looked into it. It was Sam. He opened the door, and Kaia rushed forward to hug the woman. Sam brushed past her, dodging the gesture. Kaia quickly caught up to and stopped her.

"What?" Sam sounded worn down, and her face was stained with tears.

"Where did you go?" Kaia asked.

"Out." Sam kept walking.

Dean looked at Kaia, and they shared a look of concern.

"I'll go. Take the others to the dining hall. Talk to them about what they experienced in the simulation room."

"I'll see you later." Dean replied.

Kaia caught up with Sam further down the hallway.

"We're just worried about you. You can't just go off on your own like that."

Sam spun around, her eyes burning with tears, stopping Kaia in her tracks. "You don't need to worry about me. I'm a grown ass woman, and I can take care of my-damn-self."

"I know it's just-"

"Look. It's not like I was going off to fight a war on my own. I wasn't looking for trouble."

"Then why are you strapped for it?" Kaia put as much gentleness into her voice as she could muster.

"In case trouble found me." Sam kept walking.

Kaia followed alongside her, walking in silence all the way to The Graveyard. The silence continued as they sat at Hannah's gravesite, all the while Kaia poured as much emotional comfort into her friend's mind as possible.

Two weeks passed by. Two weeks of routinely leading the twice daily B.O meetings with Dean, but never going out on the field. Two weeks of learning to use and control the abilities with the five comrades-turned-friends that she had grown so close to. Two weeks of sitting silently with Sam at Hannah's gravesite. Two weeks of preparing how to let everyone else know about them, their abilities, and their plan to end the war, once and for all.

Chapter 24

What was typically a very spacious room now seemed small and cramped. With hundreds of soldiers, men and women alike, all packed into The Lobby they were forced to stand shoulder to shoulder. No one had been sent out into the field the day or night before, and nobody knew why. Something big was about to happen, and the built up anxiety hung in the air like a stale fog as they awaited their Generals.

Kaia and Dean arrived at 6:15 am, they had requested everyone's attendance almost three hours earlier than the regularly scheduled B.O meetings, and took their place at the front of the room. They scanned the room, taking it all in before making their announcement. Close by stood the other five, and Kaia took comfort in their presence.

Dean spoke first, "So, I know you're all wondering what's going on, and to be honest I wish we could answer your questions with an easy speech that ends in a motivational war-cry, but it's a bit more complex than that. The truth always is. And you all deserve nothing less than the truth."

Dean took a pause to scan the faces in the room. Some wore confusion, some wore fear, and some wore sheer curiosity, but behind it all there was still the respect, and Dean was thankful for that.

"As you know, we weren't always here. We were refugees, escapees from Grady and his experiments, taken in by the late Aiyana Waki. May she rest in peace." Everyone's eyes floated towards her picture hanging up on the wall. It was surrounded by words she had spoken, and things she had accomplished throughout her lifetime. "But we weren't the only ones."

There were some quiet murmurs among the crowd, and Kaia took over at this point. "She had already taken in others who came from the same situation without knowing it. Some because they wanted their time with Grady to remain forgotten, others because they were forced to forget." That last statement earned many raised eyebrows. "Chris Mikami, Kurtis Gard, and Samantha Darkholme." They each stepped forward as their names were said. "There was also one other, our recently departed Hannah Adler."

Kaia glanced over to Sam, whose eyes were bright with unshed tears, and sent a wave of love washing over her.

"This is not the only information that has come to light. Two of our new recruits, Lauren Greene and Steven Rhee, are also escapees from Grady's facility."

They too stepped forward, joining the others on the dais from which Kaia and Dean addressed the crowd.

"With them they brought important information, intel that will help us put an end to this war."

The faces of the men and women before them lit up, and a feeling of hope that hadn't been felt in a long time rose among them.

"That's not all though." Kaia's voice was solemn, and it brought everyone down a notch again, "We also discovered where they came from, who built them, and why."

Dean could sense the guilt Kaia was feeling, and it broke his heart.

"Those creatures, Grady built them. He calls them his Hunters. He built them because we escaped, designed them to find people like us. When we were a part of his experimentations he implanted us with chips, and those chips acted as homing beacons for his Hunters. Words can not express how sorry we are that you have suffered on account of us. The loss of life, the exhaustion, the pain and sadness, I'm just... I'm so sorry."

Dean watched the faces in the crowd as his wife spoke, and not one of them expressed the betrayal, hatred, or anger Kaia was expecting, and he smiled.

"As she said before though, along with all that, we did find a way to end it. And part of it involves why we haven't been going out with you these past two weeks. Everyone knows Grady's history, his theories of the next step in evolution, but nobody knows just how right he was. Because he wasn't right until after the world ended. When he was no longer monitored, and could go about it as he pleased. Using methods that were torturous and atrocious at best, his fuckin' theories finally worked."

Kaia had only heard Dean curse a handful of times in the twelve years she'd known him, and all had been in the beginning, when he was an angry adolescent trapped like herself in Grady's facility. The looks that spread across the crowd were ones of shock and dismay, coupled with curiosity.

"Show 'em Sam." Kaia said.

Sam's skill in controlling and using her abilities had blown everyone else out of the water. She had proved herself time and time again in the simulations that she had mastered all of the abilities in a way that outshone them all.

Kaia tossed her Glock across to Sam, and without making a single movement, or even blinking an eye, she caught the gun mid-air with her mind. It floated around the room lazily as each component was taken apart, spread across the room, and brought back together. She held it in the air above the middle of the crowd before sending it back to Kaia, and sliding back it into its holster.

Kaia spoke before they had a chance to react, "Because of the chips Grady put in us we were unable to access all of the abilities he had brought about in us, but Dr. Seong Lee removed them for us, and for the past two weeks we have been practicing our control over them so we could have a better chance than ever before at finally defeating these Hunters."

"So what's the plan?" A voice from the crowd asked.

"About three weeks ago Dean dismembered, and brought in the body of one of the Hunters for our team to dissect and analyze. The result was that they carry within them a sphere of electricity, one of great energy, surpassing anything we've seen before. We will be executing a triangulation emp shutdown. Gi, along with Ed and his team of techs have made us equipment to perform the shutdown, and Seong has implanted our old chips into the Hunter's carcass to use as bait. Once enough of them are within range we will execute the shutdown, incapacitating them, and then use this to end it." Kaia held up a small piece of paper with numbers scribbled on it, "This is what Lauren and Steven brought back with them. It's a code that will shut the Hunter's down permanently. There is a small flap of skin located on the underside of the Hunter's jaws. Hook your finger into it and a small keyboard with ten buttons will pop out. 4 2 6 3 6 8 3 7. Game over."

Dean and Kaia stood at the head of their army facing the main doors. Between them, attached to thick handles, was the carcass of the Hunter that had started this journey. It felt like it had been much longer than the mere three weeks that had passed between now and then; it was something Dean and Kaia had reflected on the night before.

Sam, Lauren and Steven, and Kurtis and Chris stood just behind them, each carrying the three emp devices. With them stood the Colonels who would lead their squads to make sure they completed their task: Ki for Dean and Kaia, Gerard and Sasha for Sam, Amara for Lauren and Steven, and Jack for Kurtis and Chris. Those four squads were made up of fifty soldiers each, and with Ben and Freddie's scouting squad they totaled at an army of two hundred and sixty-four.

Two hundred and sixty-four men and women, versus an innumerable army of biomechanical beasts.

Ben and Freddie stood slightly off the side and ahead of Kaia and Dean, their own squad behind everyone else, awaiting orders to open the doors. Dean and Kaia looked at each other and nodded, it was time. Kaia brought a hand up to the small circular speaker that was affixed to the shoulder of her tactical jacket(now cleaned of the slime-blood from her previous outing), and pressed a small button on the side, then spoke into it.

"Alright Seong, we're ready."

A loud beep emitted from the Hunter's carcass they carried; the chips were activated. Kaia changed the frequency on the small walkie-talkie, the same one they all had, to connect back to her army. She nodded at Ben who proceeded to open the doors, and for the first time in a long time, the coppery smell of blood didn't fill the air.

They knew it was likely due to the fact that there had been no blood shed in the past twenty-four hours, but they took it as a good sign, and the fresh air reminded them of the simple pleasures the world can offer when it's not crawling with abominations.

Dean turned to face the crowd of men and women who had fought bravely over the past three years, and remembered the faces of those who weren't there, one last time.

"Let's go kill these sons-of-bitches."

The doors opened, and they all ran, heading for their assigned destinations.

"We're in position. Nothing's here yet." Chris' voice came over the walkie.

Kurtis followed with, "But we're not holding our breath."

"We've almost got the bait in position, keep your eyes peeled." Kaia said.

Soon everyone was where they needed to be, just as they'd planned, but everything was quiet.

Too quiet.

"This is real eerie guys, do you think they knew-arghh!"

The soldier standing beside Freddie was skewered, and ripped backward, leaving a trail of intestines flying through the air.

"They're here!!!" Freddie yelled, spinning around and firing into the Hunter that had just killed the first man in what was to be their bloodiest battle yet.

From where Chris and Kurtis were standing they could just see over the lip of a hill, and the color of the sunrise combined with the cumulus blurred the horizon, impeding their vision. Kurtis raised his left hand and flicked his wrist, clearing the low-lying clouds away. With the horizon easily visible they were able to see it; a swarm of Hunters climbing up the hill.

"Everyone stand your ground, we can't lose the position!" Chris yelled back to the soldiers.

Two snipers, sitting up in a large old tree, locked onto the first two Hunters that were bounding towards them.

Their synchronized shots landed in the joints of the leading limb on each, and they tumbled down, entangling themselves in one another. Several other's tripped on the unexpected obstacle, and the scene became a writhing mass of frantically kicking mechanical limbs.

"Good job guys! Keep it up!"

Sam had perched herself at the top of another old tree, just as dead looking as the others, but just as perfect for a vantage point. She saw the swarm of Hunters long before her squad did, and she wanted revenge for Hannah. Badly.

They ran in a line as opposed to crowd, using their sheer size as a tactic to eventually surround them, but they wouldn't get that far. With a flick of her wrist, all of the limbs of the Hunter's right sides span suddenly and violently, flipping up into the fleshy bodies of their neighbor. Their screeches echoed across the space between them, and everyone turned their heads at the sound. Sam's mouth twitched at the corner, satisfaction sinking in.

It was a desperate frenzy of flesh and metal as some of them managed to rip themselves free, leaving their unfortunate neighbor irreparably damaged.

Steven had jumped into the fray with the close range combatants, while Lauren had joined the line of snipers.

She never missed a shot, and with the enhanced reaction timing and heightened sense of sight she was able to fire shots off with a speed and precision that wouldn't have been humanly possible otherwise. The Hunter's limbs could be seen flying up into the air as her shots blew them off, making them much more manageable targets for the men and women below her.

The emp device was hooked onto a D-ring on her belt, ready to go as soon as she received word. As she fired a shot that prevented Steven from being unknowingly skewered she felt someone rip it from her belt. Lauren immediately swung her sniper around, cracking it into the shins of her assailant, and they toppled over, crying out in agony. Lauren stomped her boot into the small of their back and ripped the device out of their hand, clipping it back onto her belt.

Swinging the sniper over her shoulder she pulled out a side arm, crouched over the woman's body, and held it to their head.

"Turn over. Slowly." Lauren grated the words through her teeth. "Now." She pressed the barrel of the gun harder into the woman's head.

Lauren had a feeling she knew who it was, the red hair was all too easily recognizable, but she wanted to see her assailants face.

"Amara. Why?"

The woman spat at Lauren's boot, and a vicious snarl played across her face. Lauren whacked the butt of her gun against the side of Amara's head, knocking her out cold. Lauren tied her up, and laid her down on the ground in front of her. Using Amara's back Lauren propped her sniper back up, and looked for her husband through the scope. There. Lauren breathed a sigh of relief, and continued to shoot down the Hunters.

Kaia and Dean stood back to back by the bait, listening to the sounds of battle happening, but not seeing anything coming their way.

"Ben, Freddie. I need to you draw them to us. We need as many as possible in the middle of this or it won't work." Kaia said.

"Can do ." Freddie replied.

"Everybody retreat to point A! We need to draw them to the bait."

Sam had continued to toy with the Hunters as they approached. Wheeling them up into the air to come crashing down on their comrades, ripping various limbs free of the fleshy parts and driving them into different spots on their bodies, until the whole scene had become impossibly nightmarish. Gerard and Sasha looked up at Sam, both impressed and afraid of the power she exhibited.

She heard Kaia speak to Freddie over the walkie-talkie and yelled down to the squad, "Draw their attention towards point A! They need more numbers by the bait."

"What about you?" Gerard asked.

"I'm fine. Just go!" Sam said.

Gerard and Sasha shrugged at each other, then ran out into the field, the squad following close behind.

By the time Gerard and Sasha's squad had reached point A, the battle was already fierce. Ki and his squad had become one with Ben and Freddie's, while Dean and Kaia were in the middle stopping any Hunter that got too close. As soon as that bait was ripped apart the main targets would become them; at least for now they were just collateral.

Kaia caught Gerard and Sasha's squad arriving out of the corner of her eye, and with them another swarm of Hunters.

Okay guys, let's do this. Flip your devices on!

Sam flipped hers on first, easily dealing with the straggling Hunters who didn't follow the surge that chased after Gerard and Sasha.

Done.

Lauren, digging her knee deeper into the back of Amara, flipped hers on too.

Done.

No one heard anything from Chris and Kurtis.

Chris. Kurtis. What's going on? Dean asked.

There's too many of them. We were pulled away from the device, and can't get back to it.

"Ben, Freddie! Keep the fight here. Protect the bait. Chris and Kurtis are overwhelmed."

"Got it!"

Ben replied while unloaded his H&K MP5 into the face of a Hunter, and it reeled backward lunging for another man only to receive the same treatment.

Sam picked up on the transmission again. Thinking quickly she affixed her device to the topmost branch in the tree, and disguised it with a conjuring so it appeared as part of the tree itself, then sprinted towards Kurtis and Chris.

It didn't take Dean and Kaia long to reach Chris and Kurtis, and as they came in to view they were taken aback by the sight they came upon. It was a complete blood-bath. The bodies of men and women lay ripped apart, scattered all across the blood-soaked ground. Those who weren't already dead lay drowning in the pools of blood.

Kurtis and Chris, along with Jack and the last of his squad, were getting backed into a corner, formed by a steep cliff shooting straight up into the sky. The tree where the device sat was just off the side, but they had been cut off from it by the advancing Hunters.

Kaia sprinted for the device while Dean went for the remainder of Jack's squad.

Ben and Freddie had been separated from each other, and forced to retreat from the bait. They may have had the numbers with the three squads fighting together, but losing the assistance of their Generals' abilities was starting to take a toll on them. They had officially lost sight of the bait altogether, and could do nothing but fight for their lives long enough for Kaia and Dean to get the last device operational.

Freddie spotted the carcass fly up into the air, and get ripped to shreds by five Hunters, all viciously scrambling on top of each other to get at it. Once it was obliterated they all stopped at once and turned, like a flock of birds, and headed in the direction Kaia and Dean and gone. The soldiers fired at the Hunters, chasing after them, but the Hunters ignored them, knowing there was bigger fish to fry.

Sam's breath rasped in her quickly drying throat. But she kept sprinting, never faltering on her speed as she came across uprooted trees, rocks, and dismembered bodies. She pushed herself hard, but she was too late. Sam came up over the hill just in time to see it unfold in front of her eyes, like some cruel joke that she could have been there a minute earlier and prevented it all. If she had just been a little faster, she could have saved them. But she wasn't, and all she could do was watch.

Chris! Kurtis! Drop your weapons! We're gonna build a forcefield!

Dean came barreling into view, ripping one of the limbs out of the body of the Hunter in front of him as he did. As it ripped free, a large chunk of flesh tore off with it, and its gray slime-blood dripped out of the wound, curdling in the blood of the men that already soaked the ground. The Hunter screeched and scrambled backward, retreating to lick its wounds.

The three men focused all of their energy into solidifying the air so as to create a force field. The movements of the Hunters began to slow, almost as though they were trying to move through molasses. The resistance grew greater and greater until a sudden force let them move freely again. The ground vibrated with the power of the number of limbs that came crashing down upon the shield, but it held fast. The three men looked amongst themselves and laughed slightly with relief. Then, out of the corner of his eye Dean saw the worst about to happen.

The Hunter who had scrambled away had noticed Kaia setting up the final device, but she was unaware of its presence. He saw the wicked gleam on the mechanical limb that was seconds away from skewering his wife, and his mind panicked. The massive spike in distress and adrenaline forced his brain capacity into overdrive, and he teleported.

Right into the way of the attack.

A gurgled scream erupted from his lungs, and Kaia whipped around. Her face went ghost white, and her body went rigid. Tears welled in her eyes, and her heart screamed.

Dean coughed up a wad of blood, and it splattered across her face. Time, for Kaia, felt as though it had stopped mid-explosion. Everything was as nauseatingly bad as it could possibly be in that moment, and there was nothing she could do to stop it. Her eyes were wide and unblinking, filled once more with the awful vision that had haunted her for weeks.

Dean, impaled. Dead.

"Kaia..." He coughed again, reaching out towards her.

I'm sorry. His hand traced down the side of her face, tangling in her wind-whipped hair.

Kaia's mind was as frozen as her mouth.

I love you.

His hand dropped, the dead weight still hanging from her hair and resting on her chest.

Sam could only watch as her best friend's worlds shattered, and she ran for the device. Turning that on, and initiating the shutdown was their only hope of anyone surviving this right now. Sam reached them before the Hunter even had a chance to remove its death-dealing limb, and flipped it on. All at once every Hunter dropped to the ground, unmoving. In her mind's eye Sam pictured the small flap of skin under every Hunter's jaw. Raising her right hand up, and making the hook motion with her finger, the small keyboard popped out of every single one of them. Her fingers danced in the air before her as though hitting the keys, 4 2 6 3 6 8 3 7.

"Game over."

Grady's Hunters were done for good.

Chris, Kurtis, Jack, and the few soldiers remaining watched with dropped jaws as the Hunters before them fell and were finally brought to death.

Get out of here. Sam spoke into Kurtis and Chris' minds, and they were more than happy to oblige.

They hadn't yet noticed what had happened with Dean, and Sam wanted to keep it that way for now.

Sam stared at the device on the ground before her, and she could her the sharp breathing of Kaia beside her. She turned around, staying on her knees, and faced the tragedy before her.

Kaia hadn't even registered that the Hunters had stopped coming, or that Sam was right beside her. All she could concentrate on was staring into Dean's face. Only his face, for the rest of it would confirm the truth she already knew. His body was limp, held up only by the limb he was impaled on. The sparkle in his eyes that made the green so brilliant was quickly fading, becoming dull and lifeless. Blood had begun to coagulate around the corners of his mouth, and the blood that once dripped steadily enough from his fatal wound to form a puddle, had now slowed to a near halt.

Kaia's unblinking eyes had filled with enough unshed tears to completely blur her vision, and cause a sharp pain within her eyes. She refused to blink, because as soon as the tears fell she had to truly see the horror that lay before her, and the thought of that terrified her. But the pressure inevitably became too much, and she squeezed her eyes, relinquishing them of the salty liquid.

Her hand trembled as she reached out for her husband. Her voice was shaky and barely audible -a low whispery sound that almost wasn't there.

"Dean?"

Kaia shuffled herself forward until she was holding her husband's body against her chest, her legs sitting askew around him.

"Dean?"

Her voice cracked, and her face was wet with tears. They wouldn't stop coming now.

"No, no, no, no, no, no, no, no, no."

Over and over she whispered her refusal, gently rocking back and forth, and hugging his head to her chest.

Sam leaned forward to place a hand on her shoulder just as she screamed, and jumped back at the suddenness of it.

"No!"

A blast of air rippled out from her body as she screamed, shooting the limb out of Dean's body, and sending the Hunter's carcass rolling away. Dean body rocked in her arms, a dead weight that barely responded to the movement rushing past him. Kaia's body shook as the tears flowed down her face, and she pulled Dean as close to her as she could.

Sam put the walkie-talkie close to her mouth, speaking quietly into it, "Everyone return to base. The battle is over."

The two of them sat in silence, and Sam did for Kaia what she'd done for her when she'd lost Hannah. They sat until the sun set, the only sound being Kaia's whimpers, and as the final glow of the sunset dipped below the horizon Kaia finally looked up into Sam's eyes.

"Thank you."

Together they carried Dean's body back to the base.

Chapter 25

"Who's that?" Steven asked.

Lauren yanked the woman's head back by her hair -she was still out cold and didn't respond to the action.

"Amara?" Steven's shock couldn't be hidden.

"Yup. She tried to take off with the device. Ripped it off my belt while I was shooting. But I stopped her."

Lauren untied the woman's feet, and Steven helped lift her into a standing position. Keeping her hands tied at her back they each put an arm under her armpits, and dragged her back to the base.

Freddie had managed to regroup with Gerard, Ki, and Sasha, and they were ushering people back to base while scouring the ground for anyone who could still be alive. As the crowd of soldiers began to thin Freddie grew more and more worried about Ben. He started asking if anyone had seen him as they passed by, but no one had.

Freddie stepped carefully around the bodies, his boots squelching in the drenched mud as bubbles of dark blood curled up around them. As he stepped over a body that had been torn in half a scream burst forth and hand shot up from the ground, wrapping around his ankle. Instinctively he swung his weapon downwards, ready to pull the trigger, when he recognized the face.

"Ben!?"

Freddie dropped to his knees and tried to help lift his friend up, but it was no use. Ben cried out in pain, and Freddie cried out in horror. Both of his legs and left forearm had been torn off, leaving burnt and bloody entrails, and ripped flesh dangling from the wounds which had begun to coagulate with the blood that soaked the ground around him.

It was truly a horrific sight. Ben tried to speak, but it was muffled and interrupted by fits of coughing up thick blood.

"Ple- Please. Make it- make it, sto- stop."

Freddie nodded, knowing Ben was already dead. The only thing he could do now was put him out of his misery.

Freddie placed his pistol against his friend's temple, "I'm sorry brother."

Ben closed his eyes, and tears squeezed out as he said, "Thank you." It was a heart-wrenching, gurgling sound.

Freddie pulled the trigger, what was left of Ben's body went limp, and Freddie, down on one knee, wept into his arm.

The sun was close to the horizon now, and Freddie took off his jacket, laying it on the ground beside his dead friend. He lifted Ben from the ground, almost gagging at the sound his coagulated body made as it separated from the blood-soaked earth, and placed him on the jacket. Wrapping the sleeves around his mangled remains and tying them around him, Freddie gathered Ben in his arms, and carried him home.

Chris and Kurtis, with Jack and the last six in his squad, were the first to make it back. They took it upon themselves to keep track of everyone who walked back through the door, so they would know exactly who didn't make it back.

Men and Women began filing through the door, all nursing various injuries that ranged from small cuts and bruises, sprained ankles or dislocated shoulders, all the way to missing limbs.

"So that's thirty-seven from Amara's squad, but where's Amara?" Jack asked.

"Right here." Lauren said as Steven and herself dragged the unconscious woman with them.

"What are you doing?!" Jack said, rushing forward.

"She tried to take off with the device. She tried to stop us. So I stopped her." Lauren said, "Now move out of our way or you can get locked up with her."

Jack was taken aback by this stranger giving him orders, but knew he was in no position to fight her on it, so he stepped out of the way. His eyes followed them as they took Amara to a holding cell.

Hours passed as the soldiers trickled in. Twenty-eight from Gerard's squad, thirty-two from Ki and Sasha's, fifteen from Ben and Freddie's. The Colonels had come back around the same time as their remaining squad members but there was no sign of Ben or Freddie.

When they did finally see Freddie approaching the doors stomach's churned and faces cringed. Freddie was covered in thick coagulated blood, and the intensity of the smell filled the air so it was all they could taste. Freddie stopped in front of the Chris, Kurtis, and the Colonels, letting the unspoken question hang in the air.

"It's Ben."

Their eyes went wide with disbelief; he looked like a Frankenstein experiment gone wrong. As they looked closer at the face they was no denying it, this was Ben. Well, what was left of him. Freddie kept walking, heading for The Graveyard, and they watched

"I'm gonna go." Jack said, a deep sorrow in his voice.

As he left, Sasha, Gerard, and Ki followed, leaving Chris and Kurtis standing alone.

The pair slumped down the walls opposite each other, sitting by the open doors, choosing to wait for Sam, Kaia, and Dean. As the sun set, the changing colors in the sky were the only marking of time passing, and they chatted about this and that until eventually, as it always does, Claire came up.

"Have you tried talking to her lately?" Kurtis asked.

"Yeah, a couple of times. I know she's still alive, I can sense that. But I hit a brickwall every time I try. You?"

"Same." Kurtis said, adjusting his position, "I'm thinking she must have been put in a different control group or something after... you know..."

"Yeah..." Chris sighed and turned his head to look out the door.

Only the edge of the sun was visible on the horizon, and it gave everything a reddish glow. A few stars twinkled in the twilight, and the moon was full.

"I wonder where they are." Kurtis said. "Should we...? Ya know. Contact them?"

"Go for it." Chris' mind was still with Claire, and his disconnected voice showed it all too well.

Kurtis sighed and reached out to Sam, *Sam, what's going on?*

We're... busy. We'll be back soon. Just go to bed.

"Well, we've been dismissed." Kurtis jumped up.

"Thank god." Chris followed him, making sure the door was closed.

Chapter 26

"Over the past three years we have lost many people, too many... They can truly be at peace now that their deaths have finally been avenged against the creatures that have wreaked their havoc on us for so long. And I'm sure if they knew that these creatures would be discovered as creations of Grady Andrews himself they would be chuckling in their graves." Gregory's voice carried over The Graveyard easily.

The one hundred and twenty-nine survivors of the three year long war were all gathered in The Graveyard. It was a sea of blacks and grays, with Gregory at the head of it all. Several feet in front of him sat a dais, upon which the body of General Dean Whittaker was laid to rest. Kaia Whittaker stood beside him, clothed in a silk black dress, long with capped sleeves, and elegant in its simplicity. Her long hair tumbled down around her shoulders, and her eyes shone brightly from her tear-stained face.

Gathered around her were her companions: Samantha Darkholme, Lauren Greene, Steven Rhee, Chris Mikami and Kurtis Gard. One step down on the dais from them were Col. Jack Fisher, Col. Ki Cho Hyeong, Col. Sasha Ayers, Col. Gerard Barker, and Captain Freddie Barnes -who was holding an urn that housed the ashes of Captain Benjamin Payne's remains. All wore a complexion of ashen exhaustion.

"Yesterday was a victorious day, one that will be a part of our history forever. However, as it is with all great historical days, it is one of great sadness. One hundred and thirty two-soldiers lost their lives yesterday. Among them was Captain Benjamin Payne, and General Dean Whittaker. Their bravery and fortitude will never be forgotten."

Gregory paused, giving a moment of respectful silence. He glanced over at Sam, and knew what he had to do.

"There is one other, who gave her life, who was meant to be a part of this history, but it was not to be. Captain Hannah Adler. She left us two weeks ago during an attack on the base. She sacrificed her life to save the people she loved, to save the woman she loved."

Gregory met Sam's eyes and smiled at her. Throughout The Graveyard the gentle sound of falling tears, and the accompanied sniffling, could be heard. Gregory looked back up over the crowd, and finished his eulogy.

"But surviving the victories is a battle in itself. And although many of our loved ones are gone, it is us, the survivors, who will carry them with us into the future. Carry their names with us, carry their memories with us, and carry their strength with us to keep going."

Gregory stepped down and away from the dais, leaving Kaia up front and center. She looked out at the crowd for the first time since entering the funeral, and struggled to keep the tears from wracking her body.

"It has been an honor, and a privilege to fight alongside each and every one of you. The tragic losses we experienced together over the years, and yesterday alone, will never be forgotten."

Kaia was trembling, and Sam stepped up beside her, placing a comforting hand on her back. Kaia sucked in a sharp breath and composed herself, drawing strength from the comfort of her friend.

"We may have won the battle, but there is still a war to fight. Grady Andrews is still out there, and he needs to be stopped. I will only take a select few with me on this journey as it is a fight that will require the abilities that we, as Grady's subjects carry, and I can not ask you to join me. You have all given so much already, and now it is up to you to finish what Aiyana had intended to start. Rebuild. Expand outside of this base. Enjoy your lives with your friends and family, and look towards a hopeful future. "

Kaia scanned the crowd, her short burst of confident authority was already beginning to falter. She nodded tersely, forcing a smile, then took her leave without another word. Sam, Chris, Kurtis, Lauren, and Steven followed her out.

Once in the elevator Kaia spoke again, holding her posture of confident authority, but keeping her face to the doors as the tears had come again, "I'll be going to speak with Dr. Lee in the morning. I'm hoping she's found information on the best way to approach Grady's facility. I'll see you there."

The elevator doors opened, and Kaia walked briskly down the hall. All she wanted was to get behind closed doors, cry her heart out, and hopefully sleep, but Lauren caught up with her, bringing news that she didn't have the capacity to deal with in that moment.

"I'm sorry, but there's something you should know."

"What is it?" Kaia knew she sounded exasperated, and immediately apologized,"I'm sorry. What happened?"

"It's Amara. She tried to stop us from executing the triangulation. She ripped the device from my belt, she didn't succeed I stopped her, but she's locked up in a cell now."

Kaia stopped and sighed, rubbing her hands over her face and through her scalp. The stress, exhaustion, and overwhelming sadness was running her haggard. She turned to face Lauren, and her friend's heart ached at the sight of how ashen Kaia's face was.

"Find Jack and-"

"Jack wasn't too happy when he saw us drag her back inside."

"Then I'm leaving this in yours and Steven's hands for the night. Watch her. But don't talk to her. No matter what she says. If she wants to talk, let her, but I'll interrogate her tomorrow."

"Okay." Lauren hugged Kaia tightly, then rejoined Steven and relayed to him the orders.

Sam watched as Kaia made her way back to her room, desperately wanting to follow, to keep her company, and make sure she was alright. But she knew better than to be with someone who just wanted to be alone, and so she left for her own room, settling with keeping a mental watch over her friend. Just as Kaia had done for her.

Lauren and Steven had set up chairs against the wall opposite the cell that Amara was locked in. Amara was no longer unconscious but she remained silent, sitting and staring at the couple. Hours had gone by, Lauren and Steven keeping any conversation they had to themselves, and Lauren had eventually fallen asleep leaving Steven to keep the first watch of the night.

"You know, I bet I could make you feel things your little wifey there couldn't." Amara finally broke her silence, and there was a sickening level of seduction in her voice as she spoke to him.

Steven was seated leaning over, hands joined together, and elbows resting on his knees when she did. He raised an eyebrow, looking at her with disgust. Amara wriggled in the chair she was tied to, pushing her chest outwards.

"Why don't you come over here and find out. You don't even have to untie me." She tugged at her lower lip with her teeth and shook her hair out.

Steven stood up, and unlocked the cell door. The look on his face told Amara he was ready to take her, and a low chuckle emanated from her throat. As he walked over to her he reached into his back pocket and pulled out a bandana he had been using as a sweat rag during the battle yesterday. Steven stood close to the arm of the chair looking down at Amara, and she attempted to lift her bound hand. He was just out of her reach, and when the tips of her fingers managed to barely graze the material of his pants over his crotch Steven bent over, placing his hands on his knees. They were almost face to face, and as she opened her mouth to say something he stuffed the bandana into it, silencing her. He turned around and left, locking the cell door behind him. When he sat back down he saw the look on her face, and it was as disgustingly seductive as her voice was. Steven flicked his wrist, and the chair span around, leaving Amara to make googly-eyes with the wall.

Chapter 27

It was almost eleven in the morning the following day by the time everyone had made their way to dimly lit antechamber off of Seong's office -Kaia arriving last with noticeably swollen and reddened eyes. The room looked untouched since the last time they had been there, only instead of the whiteboard reading 'Project Deus', it now displayed a slightly pixelated aerial map of their old prison-home.

"Grady's facility is the only major landmark left in what was once the city of Amarillo, Texas. We-" Seong flipped to an image of a zoomed in road map with the location of their base circled on it. "are here. In what was left of Wabakimi Provincial Park after half the earth was drowned in the rising waters." Seong zoomed out on the map, revealing the distance between themselves and Grady. "Two thousand-four hundred kilometers from here to there. I will provide you with detailed maps that you can take to help you along the way. They're mostly composed of hidden backroads, but you'll also be able to find outposts that Grady has set up along the way. He's reached out further than expected, closer than expected, so don't let your guard down."

The closest outpost displayed on the board was setup within a few hundred kilometers of their base, luckily in the opposite direction of the way Lauren and Steven had approached them. To this they breathed a sigh of relief and squeezed each other's hands.

"Now I know you had worked ever so hard on making your own maps of this, but I'm sure even you'll be thankful for this find." Seong smiled at Steven as she said this, then flipped through a series of images.

They were blueprint maps showing detailed layouts of each level in the facility. Kaia stood up, and approached the whiteboard. With glossed eyes she skimmed over the details and nodded.

"This is perfect. All of it is." Kaia turned to Seong and forced a smile, "Thank you."

Sitting behind Seong were six thick zippered folder-files, and Kaia pointed towards them, "I'm assuming that's our copies?"

"Yes ma'am." Seong smiled at her.

Kaia turned to face her friends and said, "Pack up whatever you think you'll need. I'll meet back up with you for lunch, then we'll get the Rubis ready to go. We leave first thing tomorrow."

As Kaia walked out of the room Sam gently grabbed her shoulder and asked, "Where are you going?"

"To see our friend Amara."

Kaia's footsteps sounded hollow as the heels of her combat boots hit the stone steps leading to the cells. A single guard stood watch at the top of the stairs, and he nodded to her as she passed by. As soon as Kaia stepped into view, Amara's eyes were already on her, like she knew Kaia was coming.

Kaia grabbed one of the chairs left from Steven and Lauren, flipped it around so the back of it was facing Amara's cell and sat on it astride with her elbows resting on the back.

"Alright Amara, I'm gonna make this real simple for you. Tell me why you tried to stop us, what you're doing here, and who you really are, or I can just take a stroll through your mind and find what I want to know myself. And trust me, the second option will hurt. A lot. I'll make sure of it."

"Straight to business. I can appreciate that. But you can't really expect that I'll just flop over and tell you all that do you?" Amara said.

"No. In fact, I counted on you not. But I figured I'd give you the option."

Amara shrugged in response, "Alright."

"I'll start with an easy one. Who are you?"

"Why don't you try and find out."

Amara dared her with the tone of her voice, and her dark eyes bore into Kaia coldly.

"Alright. But don't say I didn't warn you."

Kaia closed her eyes, her mind quickly forming the cerebral connection that would link her mind to Amara's. The connection was instantaneous, and Kaia was running through the maze that was Amara's mind. Everything shone with an ethereal blue glow, even the cerebral figures of Amara and Kaia themselves. As Amara fled she threw various traps up: giant swinging axes, spinning blades, large boulders, and spikes that jutted up out of the ground, but Kaia dodged them effortlessly. She sprinted down thread after thread, sliding to her knees as spinning blades projected from the walls beside her, leaping into the air just in time as lethal spikes sprung forth from beneath her feet, rolling through the gaps between the weaponized pendulums. Even though her step never faltered Amara always just out of reach. Eventually, she got an idea.

Kaia kept running and dodging until there was a turn in the booby trapped maze that was Amara's mind, and instead of making the turn and following Amara down the next thread she parkoured herself off the wall, flipped over the true Amara, and landed behind her burying her Gerber combat knife to the hilt above Amara's right shoulder blade. Kaia let go, and Amara went tumbling forward, crashing into the wall, and coughed, sending a splatter of ethereal blood across the ground.

"What did I tell you?" Kaia asked.

"Well," Amara turned her head and spat out a glob of blood, "I thought you said it would be painful. You can do better than that right?"

Kaia quickly covered the space between them, and twisted the knife. The sound of the serrated edge grinding against Amara's shoulder blade was cringe-worthy, but Kaia didn't blink an eye. Amara unwillingly let out a grunt, the only sign she felt what Kaia was doing, as she twisted the handle and used it to drag Amara through the maze of her mind.

It took longer than Kaia expected for Amara to finally give in to the cries of pain she was trying so hard to hold in, and when they reached the center of the cerebral maze Kaia ripped the knife free, sending Amara sprawling, and an arc of blood splattering, across the ground.

Kaia squatted down in front of Amara, "I'm gonna ask one more time. Who are you?"

Amara spat at Kaia, and a wad of blood landed on her boot.

"You know," Kaia said, standing up and kicking the globules back towards Amara, "that's just not the answer I was looking for."

Kaia span around suddenly and punched Amara hard in the jaw, snapping her head to the left. Another gob of blood flew from Amara's mouth as her head span, and she wiped her mouth with the back of her hand before turning back to face Kaia.

"That's more like it." Amara said, a twisted pleasure in her eyes, "Come on General Whittaker. Let's see what you're made of."

Amara pulled herself up, favoring her injured shoulder, and took on an offensive stance.

"Oh sit back down."

Kaia waved her hand, and ethereal tendrils resembling vines reached out from the wall, wrapped themselves around Amara, and forced her back to the ground.

Kaia walked around the space, looking for some kind of door to the history of Amara: where she came from, who she really was, and why she was betraying them. As she looked around, her eyes fell back onto the ethereal figure of Amara.

That was her door.

Kaia stepped purposefully up to Amara's form and wrapped her hands around her head.

Back in the cell Amara's head flung back, and she let out a blood-curdling scream.

Kaia's mouth twitched, grinning in her success.

A mass of information flooded into Kaia's brain, and within seconds she knew everything.

"Thank you for your time."

Kaia nodded at Amara's limp form, then extracted herself from the maze of Amara's mind.

Kaia stood up, swinging the chair back against the wall, then entered Amara's cell. Kaia grabbed her hair, lifting the woman's head, and placed her fingers against the artery in Amara's neck. There was no pulse.

"Good riddance."

Kaia ascended the stairs with a quickened pace, stopping to let the guard know about Amara, then left to meet up with the others for lunch.

Lauren spotted Kaia as she entered the dining hall, and jogged over to meet her.

"What did you find out?"

"I think it's best if everyone hears this. And I mean everyone. The men and women she fought alongside deserve to know the truth about her."

Lauren nodded and returned to the table that her husband and friends were seated at.

Kaia walked past Jack on her way to the head of the room, and she sympathized with the worry in his eyes.

"If I can get everyone's attention please!"

Kaia's voice carried over the room, silencing the many conversations that were happening. All eyes were on her, Jack's more intense than the others, and her own eyes softened at the concern lying within them. With that soft look, Jack knew his entire opinion of the woman he was starting to fall in love with was about to be altered forever.

"Colonel Amara Juana, as most of you grew to know, was a brave and beautiful woman. Full of spirit and charm. But it was all a lie." Kaia's eyes landed on Jack again, and he was rigid in his chair.

"She was a youth that Grady had taken under his wing -an apprentice of sorts- and she assisted him in the unethical conduct of his ways behind closed doors."

Kaia let out a short exasperated sigh, almost a chuckle, "Closed doors is right. I don't remember seeing her face once. Anyways, she was sent here to find us. Myself, Chris, Kurtis, Sam, Hannah, and Dean." Kaia's voice cracked when she said her dearly departed's name, and Sam's heart lurched.

"I don't know why she stayed for as long as she did, and I don't understand why she didn't turn us over to him, but what I do know is that she did try to help his Hunters take this place down. She orchestrated the attack that myself and Dean found our Colonels trapped in three weeks ago, as well as the attack on the base that led to Hannah's death. She also attacked Lauren in an attempt to stop us from completing the shutdown. And that's just to name a few."

Jack felt like he had been kicked while he was already down, unable to comprehend that it was her doing that gave those Hunter's their military tactics that day.

"Unfortunately I was not able to retrieve this information easily. She fought me, and it led to her end. I am sorry for those of you who had grown close with her, but she was a traitor."

No one questioned that what Kaia said was the truth, and she took their silence as acceptance. Those who weren't close with her held faces of empathetic sadness, while those who had grown to know who she claimed to be struggled with the emotions bubbling to the surface. Jack, on the other hand, looked devastated, and Kaia felt for him. As she headed towards her table she stopped and placed a hand on Jack's shoulder.

"I'm so sorry."

Jack stared straight ahead, and Kaia gave his shoulder a comforting squeeze then left. She sat down beside Sam, and dropped her head into her hands sighing.

"Let's just eat, then get to packing up the Rubis." Kaia said before anyone could ask or say anything.

Three out of the ten old Rubicons were lined up in front of the large garage door, the once shiny platinum 'Jeep' logo decals had rusted to a reddish brown.

Kaia tossed one last bag into her vehicle, then went down the lineup to do a final double check. As she turned around she almost ran right into Jack. Ki, Sasha, Gerard, and Freddie were right behind him, and they all stifled a chuckle at the look of shock that came across their Generals' face.

"Holy shit!"

Kaia's hand flew to her mouth, and she genuinely smiled for the first time since Dean died in front of her.

"You nearly scared me half to death."

"Sorry Mrs. Whittaker."

Kaia's smile died, and immediately Jack recoiled at what he had just said.

"Oh no. I'm so sorry. I didn't mean to. I just. Ah, fuck."

Jack rubbed his head, his facial expression showing just how much of an idiot he felt he had been in that moment.

"It's okay. There's no need for titles anymore, of any kind. It's just Kaia now." She made that forced smile again, and her eyes shone with the threat of fresh tears, but she held them back. "What can I do for you?"

"Well, we came here because... Look, I know you don't want anyone risking their lives anymore, and I know the battle on our homefront is over, but we're signed up til the end, and if I'm being honest I've got some issues that I'd like to address with Mr. Grady Andrews and his accomplices."

Kaia made to protest, but decided against it. "We'll get another Rubi packed up. Meet us back here first thing tomorrow morning."

"We'll see you then. Kaia." Jack smiled and nodded, then left with the other ex-Colonels/Captain.

Epilogue

"What happened?!" Grady's voice boomed through Amara's earpiece, "I should leave you out for the crows to pick at."

Amara sat camouflaged on the roof, braiding her hair like it was a lazy Sunday afternoon, and watched as Kaia and her group drove away.

"Look, I tried to stop Aiyana's pitiful army, but they're not quite as pitiful as we thought. You just have to accept the fact that your Hunters are done with."

She could hear his breath seething between his teeth, and she grinned.

"I almost died you know, trying to stop them" Amara spoke nonchalantly as she picked dirt out from under her nails. "My conjuring is getting better. They couldn't even tell the difference between my pulse and the fake one, let alone the guard I placed at my watch after I disposed of theirs."

"You always were my star pupil." Grady said.

She could practically feel the pride emanating from his voice.

"Yeah. So remember that next time you try to threaten me."

Grady was never phased by her sudden changes in demeanor, he knew he'd always have the upper hand when it came to his little underling.

"Never mind that." He said, shrugging her off, "Has there been any sign of Kaia and the others? I'm having a hard time believing that regular soldiers could take down my Hunters."

"Nope. No Kaia. No Dean. No Chris. No Kurtis. No Lauren. No Steven."

"Well they must be hiding somewhere!"

"Calm down before you give yourself an aneurysm."

Amara stood up as the Rubicons began to fade into the distance, and the small braid that always hung from the right of her head danced in the breeze.

"Just. Find them."

Static followed his command, signifying that he had hung up on her, and Amara watched as the last Rubicon disappeared from view. She wasn't sure why she listened to that voice that told her not to tell him that she knew exactly where all of them were, and that somehow Samantha and Hannah had survived the swipe -well, only

Samantha now. But it was as nagging as it was instinctual, and on some level she trusted it more than him, so she kept the information to herself. For now.

Thank you reader!

I hope you enjoyed reading the journey
as much as I enjoyed writing it! :)

For more info on me and my upcoming projects
head over to https://zoelecraw.wixsite.com/author

Follow me on your favorite social media

Instagram @zoelecraw

Twitter @ZoeLeCraw

Facebook Page @zoeelecraw

CPSIA information can be obtained
at www.ICGtesting.com
Printed in the USA
LVOW03s2039200418
574338LV00005B/6/P

9 781773 029436